The Secret of Zen Ducks

The Secret of Zen Ducks

by

Robert Frauenhofer

ISBN: 0-75960-096-1

1stBooks -rev. 10/09/00

Thanks to Jim Anderson without whom this would not have been written.

jyop

Author's Note

You are about to read the most important novel of the century. If that sounds bold or foolish, try this:

We are on the threshold of the most exciting times in the history of mankind. **The rich will get richer, the middle class will live as the rich do now, and the poor will be raised to the level of the middle class.** Furthermore, the lifespan will be extended and vitality enjoyed into very old age.

Our task now is to step over the threshold, and enter a world we may not comprehend. If you "get it", the secret of the ducks will be revealed, and you will be thrilled, for it is an epiphany from which your vision of the world will be changed forever.

Until our society fully grasps the meaning of Zen Ducks, we cannot become a truly advanced civilization.

It is said that the mind cannot hear until the heart listens. Listen with your heart, and a beam of light will pierce the darkness of your mind. In an age searching for a new myth, you will find a new reality.

.

Party Time

Is that all there is?
Then pour the drinks,
and let's party.

*H*urry! Get your jollys before it's too late. If you miss out, you'll die angry and bitter.

How dreadful it is to die and be nothing forever. At least, if we get a few kicks in the short time we're here, we can face death satisfied with our little pleasures.

But is that it? Is that all there is?

There was a boy who knew the answer; but when he said it, ears did not hear: imagine trying to describe meaning to an age born to the darkness of meaninglessness. It's like trying to describe the beauty of a sunset, or the thrill of soul-stirring music to a person who was born deaf and blind.

Modern man has expanded his awareness and enriched his life through education, art, music and good health. Yet, all of these accomplishments have led to a dead end.

Where do we turn in our despair? Who will lead us? Can we turn to wise old men, politicians, religious leaders?

The little boy sat down on a couch when a cricket jumped onto his lap. He grabbed him in the palm of his hand, and carried him outside. The feel of the cricket jumping around in his cupped hand was a sensation which no adult could know. He set the black, shiny bug on the grass, and told him to stay out there with his friends.

Then one day, as he raked leaves, wasps buzzed slowly around his face. Somehow, he knew they meant no harm, so he kept working. One landed on his shirtless back, then one on his shoulder; they landed and departed like 747's from a runway. They did not feel like flies which have a prickly feel; they walked softly, their legs felt like the touch of a feather. He

1

sensed that they sensed he was friendly, and they were welcome to his sweat if that's what they wanted.

Another incident occurred on a beach when he saw a sea gull tangled in a fishing line. As children approached, a lady said, "No! They bite; they're dirty birds. You can get rabies."

But the boy picked it up, unconcerned, as the crowd moaned. He heard gasps as the gull nipped at his arms with its sharp beak; but it only took a few seconds for the bird to realize it was safe. It waited patiently as the kids untangled it. Finally, he released it into the air, and the kids waved goodbye.

The feel of the bird's warm body against his chest was the same as the touch of the wasps, which was the same as the feel of the cricket in his hand.

It was hard to listen to a boy when he talked about bugs and birds. Adults chuckled or smiled wearily as they listened, but did not hear. They looked at him with frustration knowing he could not comprehend their wisdom and experience.

He looked at them as if something were missing.

They would not listen to a boy when they could listen instead to the despair of the disillusioned: A celebrity described how he felt one day as he drove his car. He observed that the road ahead looked narrow, but widened out as he approached. It suddenly occurred to him that fame was just the opposite. From a distance, it looked great, but as you came closer, it diminished. That was the point where the rich and famous turned to drugs and sang: Is that all there is?

To cope with the feeling of powerlessness as life slipped away, they cracked out the booze and had a party.

This is the philosophy of despair, the religion of our time. It's too much to ask the deaf and blind to believe in music and beauty; it's too much to ask educated, sophisticated adults to believe in a meaningful universe.

But when the party's over, ask the boy: is that all there is?

He will say, "No, there's more ... much more. Come closer, and I will tell you."

As you bend down to listen, you must not condescend, for the answer he gives is much more profound than you can comprehend, or even imagine.

"Of course that's not all there is."

"Then what else is there?"

"The crickets ... the bees ... the birds."

Robert Frauenhofer

Bloody Money

Religion is dead?
So it has been said.
Does a snake not shed its skin
Its growth once more to begin?

*I*t was the year 2020, the most exciting time ever to be alive. A secret slowly revealed itself like a flower pushing up between weeds, a secret so awesome it could transform the 21st century into a time of awakening and joy, or hasten the coming of Armageddon.

Sarah Figueroa heard the secret deep in her soul; but the sound was indistinguishable like a whisper muffled by the wind. She was reluctant to talk to Don about it even though they had been married for 15 years. He did not ... could not understand.

He lived in a common sense world, "commonsenseville" Sarah called it, where people were not supposed to have profound insights.

"Einstein!" she would argue. "What he discovered doesn't make sense, common sense that is."

"Well, that's the exception," was his dismissal.

He teased her about her "feelings"; but she knew he meant no disrespect. Still, when it came to this, she was more sensitive than she let on, and wished he had never told a friend about it. When word got around about "Sarah's secret", it made her sound like some kind of kook.

She would walk into a room and people would stop laughing and try to be polite. At the school where she taught, kids would say things loud enough for her to hear, laugh, and walk away. Sometimes the ridicule turned ugly and cruel.

Now she had to prove she was not crazy.

5

And yet, even the kids and their cruel jokes, or Don's teasing didn't matter to her compared to the derision from her own peers. Catty remarks and sneers really got under her skin.

One day at a teacher's meeting as they discussed a problem with the students, a teacher said, "Perhaps Mrs. Figeuroa could offer a solution. One of her ... ephiphanies ... would surely solve the problem."

It was supposed to be a joke, but the laughter was derisive and vicious. When she tried to respond, they waved it off in a show of superiority.

Don and his big mouth.

He was an average guy who felt obliged to live in commonsenseville where it was easier to get along in an environment of W.Y.S.I.W.Y.G.: what you see is what you get.

But Sarah saw much more. When she stared at a flower, she saw planets colliding; Don saw petals on a stick. When she gazed at a mountain, she saw the face of God; Don saw a pile of rocks.

Yet, in spite of his dismissals, there were times when he was overwhelmed by a torment within. He wondered how anyone could ever be content with life when he experienced this passion, this ... yearning. What was it he wanted? What would satisfy him? He had everything a man could ask for: an elegant home in Mill Valley, lovely wife and two kids, good friends, and a lucrative contracting business.

Some people are builders, some are destroyers: Don was a builder from the day he was born. Every new project was exciting and rewarding; yet, he felt unfulfilled. With all the power of his mind, all the strength in his muscles, with his entire spirit he wanted to ... to do what? What was the ache in his heart, where did it come from?

He thought about the strange things happening in the Bay Area; but saw no connection to the stirring in his soul. Murder, suicides, he dismissed it all as a passing wave of unexplained phenomena and hysteria. Mysterious events which always happened on or in the vicinity of the Golden Gate Bridge signaled the coming of the age of Aquarius, an age as powerful and incomprehensible as the rising sun ... and just as inevitable; but ears did not hear these signals, nor did eyes see.

It was a beautiful Saturday morning in the Bay Area as Don sat in the kitchen staring at the "Chron" on the table. He was only half awake, but he bounced to his feet as a rock crashed through the window. He ran toward the door as Sarah rushed in, still in panties and no bra.

"No, Don! Don't let them provoke you!"

He looked at his shotgun. "I'm sick and tired of these people ..."

"No! Think about the kids! I don't want anybody hurt."

"Bastards! Can't they see we don't have the money?" He ignored her and ran out to confront the two hecklers, shotgun in hand.

A big man with a flat nose and hideous face stepped in front of a very pale, thin man as if to protect him. For a moment, Don hesitated, not out of fear, but surprise at the extreme ugliness of the man. Never had he seen such a repulsive face; it almost seemed to ooze with pus.

"It's OK, Herb." The effeminate lips spoke softly and articulately as he looked into Don's eyes. "You're not going to use that thing."

"Try me, asshole."

"The name is Sean. I advise you to use it." He glanced up at Herb as if to indicate that the sheer size and ugliness of this man commanded more respect.

"You got no right to that money!" Herb shouted.

"I don't have the damn money!" Don replied, frustration in his voice. "I don't even want it. I just want to be left alone."

"Yeah, right, you don't want it," Herb said as he started to circle slowly.

Sean tried to divert Don's attention. "Sir, we know you have it. Why don't you just save yourself and your family a lot of grief, and ..."

Don saw what they were up to and fired a shot in the air.

7

"Hey!"

"Next one's up your ass."

Herb looked with pleasure as Sarah opened the door and pleaded with Don.

"No, Don. Don't shoot that thing!"

As he turned toward her, Herb jumped at his chance and grabbed the gun. He held it under Don's chin as he shouted, "get your tight little ass out here or I'll blow his head off!"

She was so afraid for Don that she forgot she was half naked and walked obediently toward them. "Please, no."

Suddenly, without a sound, two men wearing expensive suits walked up the driveway behind Herb and pointed guns at Sean.

"Drop it or I blow your friend into next week."

"Huh? The mob? Where'd you come from?"

Herb quickly dropped the shotgun and let Sean do the talking.

"It's OK, Herb, they stopped us for now."

"Now and forever, pyuke face," one of the men said as he put a gun to Sean's nose. "You touch that money, and we come after you."

"Don't call my friend names," Herb replied angrily.

"I'll call him what I want. His face looks like somebody pyuked all over it. Pyuke face! Go ahead, big man. Stop me!"

"No, Herb. Let's go." He looked at Don and said, "I would sleep with that thing if I were you. Ungh ... don't push. We're gone."

As they walked toward their car, Herb looked back at Don and said, "You ain't gonna live long enough to use that money."

"Get outa my face you ugly goon!" Don was angry, but relieved. He'd never had a shotgun in his chin before.

Herb was ballistic; he was especially sensitive about his very ugly face.

"You should not have said that," Sean said as he put his hand to Herb's chest to hold him back. "I pity you. You should have thought about your family."

"What! You son of a ..."

8

"No Don." Sarah grabbed his hand to hold him back.

As they left, she scolded, "Now you've done it. Did you have to use that damn gun? If it weren't for these two men here ..." She put her hands over her breasts self consciously.

"Just protecting our investment, ma'am."

Don pleaded. "Can't you guys get it through your head? We don't have the money! Tell your boss to give up."

"That ain't gonna happen. He knows you talked to Zack; you were in on it. Zack owed us a lot of money; now you owe us a lot of money. Lucky for you we were sitting in the car behind the shrubs just now; and that's where we're gonna stay ... for as long as it takes."

It all started when a body was found floating south of the Cliff House, the right hand severed. It was Zack Pinches, a city official under investigation after it was discovered that thirteen million dollars of city funds could not be accounted for. The hand was discovered in a pool of blood next to the rail on the Golden Gate Bridge. Fort Point, under the bridge on the city side, was close to the area where his body must have hit the water. Baker Beach was just down the coast in sight of the bridge, separated by wooded areas where hikers shared an ideal setting with tourists. Thick stands of Monterey Cypress provided perfect cover for potential rapists and murderers. Newcomers often talked about the eerie feeling they got as they walked through the tunnels of evergreens as fog drifted and swirled.

Zack lived in a home overlooking Baker Beach where his car had been left in the garage on the night of his death. Police theorized that he had tried to stash the money because he was being pursued. He must have had a briefcase handcuffed to his wrist; his pursuers were in a hurry and chopped his hand off before they threw him over the side. But a briefcase would not hold that much money, where was the rest?

A note found in his pocket indicated that he must have had an accomplice. He didn't want to be caught with a map, or instructions to find it; so he wrote a riddle in a language only an accomplice would have understood: 'The baker pointed to the top shelf in his case and said, a baker's dozen is thirteen'. This could only mean thirteen million dollars was stashed somewhere near Baker Beach, but it would take someone he knew to understand what he meant by the top shelf.

When word got out about the note, the press had a field day. Headlines proclaimed: 'LATEST CLUE', and cleared newspapers off the shelves. Treasure hunters swarmed the area, some brazen enough to bring fold-up shovels. Fights broke out as people tried to hold their positions, as if they had staked a claim. The mayor finally convinced everyone of the "facts of life": the area had been thoroughly searched; the money could not be there, and if it was, they couldn't keep it. The police chief had made it clear: the law would come down hard on anyone who tried to take it; but people persisted as they do when that much money is involved.

Even as they searched, they could not get their minds off the bridge. It seemed to be watching over them as they glanced self-consciously at the towers like children sneaking behind their mother's back. They did not realize it was the center of a much greater mystery than the death of Zack Pinches. It was a mystery whose secret could not be told.

Don and Sarah were part of that mystery, and tried to understand how they had gotten involved. She was dressed now, and the kids were awake watching TV.

"Life was so simple," Don said, wishing it would all go away. "Just because of that jerk ... that biker on the bridge."

They had been on the bridge when a homeless man stopped near the rail close to where they stood looking at the San Francisco skyline. He climbed the rail in an attempt to commit suicide, but hesitated just long enough for Don to grab him by the waist and pull him down. His army jacket opened, and one humdred dollar bills fell out. The wind churned the bills into a swirling cloud of paper which seemed to grow thicker as bills peeled from large wads of cash on the ground. Tourists grabbed for the money, but the wind was too strong. Bills flew everywhere, splashing against windshields of cars speeding across the bridge. Don let go of the man and grabbed wads of cash before they could blow away. Free from Don's grasp, he quickly stood up, took the jacket off, threw it in the air, and leaped over the rail to his death. More wads of money landed in Don's lap as he kneeled on the ground reaching for the man and looking at the money in a state of confusion.

Tourists taunted him for keeping the money for himself; but he explained that he would hold it until the police came.

"Yeah, right!" A young man bellowed for all to hear. "You're in on it. I saw the whole thing. That guy was giving you the money."

TV crews showed up with the police who questioned Don and Sarah, and held the money pending an investigation.

Reporters were anxious to follow up on the accusations of the young biker who made it a point to inform them of his suspicions. By the time they finished their interview with Don and Sarah, they had convinced viewers nationwide that this well-to-do couple from Mill Valley were involved in the disappearance of the money.

"So now ..." Sarah suffered her emotions as she spoke, "now we have to fight this ... this war. Everybody thinks we have it."

"It just goes to show how people can invent things," Don said with a sneer. He had never been a cynic until now. "I only talked to that Zack ... whatever his name is ... one time. I didn't even know who he was until he told me."

He had been seen talking to Zack at Don's favorite coffee shop. It was a chance meeting; they were elbow to elbow at the counter and started to talk about the news. Somebody remembered that and the press never forgot it.

"I know you're not linked to him in any way," Sarah said, and then realized it should not have been necessary to say it. "I mean, just because of some stupid newspaper articles. They're just trying to make a case so they can sell newspapers. Everybody in San Francisco thinks they saw you and him in some coffee shop together. I know better."

"Well, it's nice to know my wife doesn't think I stole thirteen million dollars."

"But I have this strange feeling," she said as she looked out the window. "We're not just spectators in this whole thing. We're involved."

"Maybe, but the next guy who throws a rock through my window, or threatens my kids ..."

"No. Let the cops handle it."

"The cops? Sure. They think we have it, too. And the mob ... and our neighbors. We had a great life. Then, all of a sudden some guy throws money around and jumps off the bridge. Spark. He had to be a Spark."

Suicide by fire had become common nationwide. A reporter at the scene of the charred remains of a suicide remarked sarcastically, "I guess you might say he sparked our attention."

The name caught on; those who chose death by fire became known as "Sparks". Like sparks, their glory was intense, but brief.

For intellectuals, only a sophisticated explanation would do. A psychiatrist tried to explain: "It seems to be the mentality of new age people; they do things that can't be explained by anything other than the values imprinted on the collective unconscious. Like teen-agers they're determined to do their own thing; and when we provide an explanation for their behavior, they deliberately do something else. Sparks are simply the ultimate rebellion."

Sarah wondered out loud. "Maybe we're connected somehow to this whole mystery, just like the Sparks."

"Sparks? We ... us ... what? The Sparks are all nuts." He quickly dismissed it.

"But why are there so many of them? What's happening? She changed her pace and became assertive. "Just like everything else happening in the world. It's so simple, and all those big brains can't figure it out. Nobody would listen to an ordinary person like me. What do I know?"

"I have no idea," he said, bewildered and unable to accept her gut feelings. She always said it came from the heart: some things you know; some things you just feel. "So what do you know?" he asked argumentatively. "Tell me. Go ahead. What do you know? Do you know what life is all about? You have all the answers?"

"Yes."

"Uh ... what? Sarah ..."

"Beyond this world, no. But I know what's happening in the world today, and all those big brains can't figure it out. And if you could figure it out, you would never be unhappy again."

"Who said I'm not ... what are you saying?"

"Oh, Don, I know you're basically happy most of the time, but there are times when you go down inside and find a dark place where you seem to be, well ... not depressed, but like a child lost in the woods."

"But that's normal. Nobody is up all the time." He was upset by her words, but tried to show how reasonable he was.

She saw through his denial and said, "Yes, but for you it's deep. You feel like something is missing."

She was right, and he knew it; something was out of synch.

"O.K., O.K. I'll play your game." He was beginning to lose it. She had him on the edge, and he didn't like it. "Suppose you're right. Something is missing. What is it?"

"There's something you have to do."

"What?"

"I don't know."

"Hokeefine."

"Oh, sure. End of discussion, right? When you say hokeefine, that's it. It's over."

"You just ended it, not me. You're the one who knows everything."

"I know one thing, I know there's something going on inside you. Yes, you're just an average family man who loves his wife and kids, you work hard in your contracting business, and you're basically happy. But there's more. What is it? Why don't you share it?" She goaded him until he became defensive.

"But, Sare, don't we all feel a kind of ... emptiness. Nobody knows what life is all about."

"I do ... sort of."

"Oh, excuuuse me, I forgot. Sarah's secret. You know more than all those scientists and professors. Maybe you watch too many of those debates on TV."

He referred to the weekly debates by scientists, politicians, and religious leaders. They seemed to be watching a gigantic clock ticking down to the final second as they worried over global warming, overpopulation, oil depletion, urban sprawl, environmental destruction, and crime. They talked about "THE COUNT" which had been developed as a measure of these factors, and as a guide to economic management. When the count was above 90, it was a warning, like a smog alert. It was clear that we would slowly lose our freedom if we could not keep the count below 90. The year 2020 had seen the count rise to 96; it had turned into a bloody year marred by riots and chaos.

Too many criminals were incarcerated in the 90's and the first decade of the 21st century. Now, they were being released as their time was up. This created a subculture of desperate people who, joined by others who had fallen through the cracks, seemed to be everywhere.

In the meantime, overpopulation had created a demand for greater restrictions on growth; Californians were polarized in the fight to end immigration completely, and to restrict unnecessary driving. Oil resources could not last forever, and no progress had been made in producing more efficient fuels, even as the number of cars continued to grow endlessly. Gas prices were at $8.99 per gallon and rising; but the oil companies and auto makers loved it. Most people believed it was necessary to keep the economy going; others warned: something's got to give.

Intellectuals argued endlessly: An economist said the world had become like a house of cards. You stack the cards two at a time hoping that each section will hold its own independently of all the rest; but you know the longer it goes on, and the bigger it gets, the more sensitive it becomes to the slightest touch. Someday, it will all collapse ... not a little at a time, not in waves, but all at once.

A psychiatrist said the riots were based on hopelessness. He called it the storm-the-castle syndrome. When the haves get richer and more powerful, and the have-nots get poorer and more desperate, there comes a point where life is intolerable. Without regard for their own safety, they simply say, 'go ahead, kill us all. It doesn't matter anymore'. Rioters become so angry and bitter, they develop a greater desire to destroy than to live. The vengeance seeker no longer cares about love, life or happiness; his love, life and happiness *is* revenge.

Massive riots had become planned, organized uprisings as opposed to the spontaneous outbursts of the past. Black leaders warned that civil war could erupt on a hit-and-run basis if discrimination did not end; and poor people of all races would participate.

But the haves responded true to form.

Law-and-order! Law-and-order!

We stood on the line between riot and civil war, and we knew we had to make a decision. If we crossed the line, the new civil war would not be soldiers lined up on battlefields; it would be a police state with 'our' gangs against 'theirs'. We would call our guys SWAT teams and theirs street gangs; we were the National Guard, they were rioters and looters; we were justified, they were not.

If the new age was about to begin, then the question we had to answer was: would it be an age of darkness or light? We had to make the choice together.

Choice!

As always, choices seem to get more complicated just as we are about to bring them into focus. They were the same choices as always ... life or death, good or evil; but now, with the latest developments in medical and nutritional science, a centenarian could expect to have the strength and vitality of a thirty year-old. These developments further polarized the haves and have-nots as the increase in population caused greater competition for wealth. As China and other previously low consumer nations made tremendous demands on oil and other natural resources, it became apparent that the choice would come down to who shall live, you or me. We thought the civilized world had overcome the law of the jungle: kill or be killed. Now we could be moving back in that direction, only on a massive scale. In an effort to avoid the inevitable, petitions had been started to propose a bill to require mandatory birth control.

But there was something else ... something about the choice we had never known, and had never wanted to know.

Sarah knew, but she would not provoke Don further.

It was a beautiful spring day, and he wanted to enjoy San Francisco with his family in spite of the risk. He would pack a gun in the van, and live his normal life in defiance of all those idiots who harassed him over money he did not have.

He opened the window and shouted, "Yaahooooo! You sons-a-bitches! You're not stoppin' me."

Kevin, a twelve year-old, walked into the kitchen shaking his head.

"Daddo, daddo."

He felt a close bond with Don when he called him Daddo; and he was the only one Don called Kiddo. It was a special respect for this pseudo genius who wore glasses and played the role with delight. He was a perfect example of the power of identity. He believed he was brilliant; therefore, his teachers believed he was brilliant; therefore, he was brilliant.

He always spoke articulately except when he joked around with his dad; he jumped up and down in response to Don's scream.

It was typical for Kevin. Like Don, he had a wild streak which often got him in trouble; yet, he could be well-behaved and studious.

Candace, the younger of two children, spoke in a strong, quacking voice, as she bounced into the room. "Dad's goin' bonkers again."

"That's OK, Candy; I like bonkers."

"Oh, dad." Her eyes twinkled.

"Oh, dad-o-dad-o-dad," he mocked as he sat his tall muscular frame down and hunched over the morning paper. He ignored Kevin's stare as he turned the pages.

"Dad! Are we going to Crissy Field? I want to fly my kite!"

"Looks like I got a window to fix first."

Sarah intervened. "Windows can wait. Give your dad a hug-a-bug and maybe he'll ..."

"Oh, mom."

Don looked away from the newspaper and stared at Kevin who replied submissively, "Oh, dad."

Don feigned a mean face, and spoke in a deep voice. "You're never too old for a hug-a-bug."

Kevin hugged Don as he said, "Hug-a-bugga-bugga."

"What else?" Don demanded.

Kevin put the point of his nose to the point of Don's nose.

"O.K., what was the question?"

"Why do I still have to hugabug every day?"

"I told you, I don't care what the rest of the world does; this family still knows the meaning of affection."

"Dad, I just want to fly my kite."

"Which kite?" Sarah asked angrily. "I hope you don't still have that thing. After the trouble we had over that ..."

"Mom. I put it away."

"I thought you destroyed it. You were supposed to get rid of it."

"I did. It's in the garage ... up over the ..."

"You call that getting rid of it? I still can't believe you did such a thing."

"Oh, ma."

"Don't oh ma me. If I ever ..."

"Sare," Don said without raising his head from the newspaper. "Is this the article you wanted me to read?"

"The Mac Rogers column. Carol told me to look for it. I haven't read it yet." She continued to scold Kevin as Don consumed the article hungrily.

He liked "Big Mac" Rogers, and looked forward to his weekly column. During the week, he often listened to Mac's radio talk show.

"Listen to this," Don said, enthusiastically. . "'I was stranded on the plains, lost and alone. I walked and walked until my head drooped down. As I watched for obstacles at my feet, I noticed ...'"

"Is this about the money?" Kevin asked.

Sarah jerked her head, and stared at him angrily. "I told you I don't want to hear any more about that money. We're in enough trouble ..."

"Will you just listen? This is great ... inspiring! So anyway, he's stranded on the plains ..."

"Who?"

"Mac Rogers. It doesn't matter who. Just listen. 'As I watched for obstacles at my feet, I noticed some dead plants. I could not tell what kind of plants they were; they were wilted so badly. Only nature's miracle could have germinated their seeds in this desolate place.'"

"Dad, why don't you tell the one about the secret of life?"

"Not now, Kev."

"But you never finished it."

"Just listen, OK? 'I flopped down to rest as I looked back at where I had been. I had covered miles of lifeless plains ... I would perish. I got up and started walking again, head down, listless, hopeless. For some reason, I kept looking at those dried up plants. There were more of them now, and they seemed to have a little more life in them.

'Could it be ... I ran to the top of a knoll and looked ahead as far as the eye could see. There, in the distance, was a great forest; my pace quickened. As I approached the trees, I noticed those wretched plants were not so dismal now. They were healthy, and their leaves told me they were azaleas. Finally, in the forest, there was life, water, berries. I knew I would survive.'"

"Dad, why are you reading this to us?" Candy was bored.

"Because it's inspiring, it's eloquent, it's ... you wouldn't understand. Just listen.

'I saw azaleas in full bloom. They were vigorous with shiny leaves and succulent stems; the flowers were as brilliant as fire. Azaleas are native to forests where they get filtered light, cool misty air, and light soil covered with humus from the trees. These conditions are conducive to lush, vibrant plants.

'We are living in the most exciting times the human race has ever known; our potential is beyond our imagination. In the decades ahead, the rich can get richer; the middle class can live as the rich live now; and the poor can enjoy the lifestyle of today's middle class. There is great hope for the future, not despair. We will grow food from cultures almost without limits; we will extend youth and life expectancy even further; technology will continue to astound us."

Don raised his voice and talked faster.

"'But there are those who say Armageddon is upon us. They look back at the history of mankind and despair. They point to over five-thousand wars, torture, hatred, bigotry and ignorance, and give up all hope for this lunatic race of humankind.

'They are as I was when I walked the plains in fear of death. But instead of looking back at where we have been, they need to look forward to where we *can* be.

'We are standing now at the edge of a great forest filled with life, beauty and vitality. We should be thrilled!

'Yes, we have a history of violence and ignorance; but like the azaleas struggling to survive on the plains, we have never lived in our truly native habitat ... our garden of Eden. There, we

19

will find conditions conducive to growth, vitality, joy, beauty, love.

'Skeptics need only look at the good we have accomplished: music, science, technology, medicine, poetry, agriculture, travel. Great people, genius, and insight have provided the energy to get us here ... here and now at the edge of the forest. OUR TASK NOW IS TO ENTER..

'There is a way into this forest ... a path. Stay tuned to this column.'"

Sarah said nothing.

"Well?"

"I love it."

"But?"

"But ... well ... people will say it's naive, Utopian."

"Maybe that's true, but the path ... the pyramid. What does it really mean?" He knew, intuitively, it had something to do with the stirring in his soul.

"It's not necessary to discuss it. In fact, it's not necessary to do anything ... except get out of the way and let it happen."

"But if people could only ..."

"Let's get ready," she interrupted. "I want to go back ... I'm not afraid. And they're not going to stop me from having a picnic with my kids. It's Saturday. My bridge awaits."

Sarah had a thing about the Golden Gate Bridge. Raised in a small town in Connecticut, she had always looked forward to the day when she would walk across the famous Golden Gate. Now she lived in Mill Valley within minutes of her beloved bridge. She would stand on the span and gaze at the beauty of the San Francisco skyline as the wind blew her hair in all directions. She couldn't get enough of the excitement which seemed to be built into this place.

At thirty-four, she was more than sexy, she was charming and magnetic. Her smooth voluptuous figure was a delight to behold as she walked with natural grace and dignity. Her long, flowing, black hair, and dark eyes, made heads turn and stare with curiosity and admiration.

There was something about her ... maybe it was spiritual ... what ever it was, it made you forget her face even as you admired the beauty of it. Like looking through glass at a work of art, you looked through her face and saw her soul.

She had given up teaching when she found herself in conflict with her peers. It all started when she heard some people talking about sex education:

'Teenagers don't make love, they just screw; they're no different than my German Shepherd. They only see the physical side of sex.'

Sarah knew instantly, and perhaps instinctively, there was something wrong with that statement. She felt confused for the first time in her life.

Confusion can be the beginning of wisdom.

Where had she heard that before? Must have been one of Mac Rogers' gems.

That night, she did some soul searching, and woke up the next day more confused than ever.

She went to a park with a loaf of bread to feed the ducks. As she walked toward the pond, they saw her coming, and the whole flock waddled quickly toward her. They quacked and quacked as she distributed the bread. Some were so aggressive, they stepped on her feet to get closer. She scooped down to feed them, and suddenly the world seemed to stand still. As she looked into their eyes, she saw something strange ... no, not strange ... mysterious ... no, there is no word for it. She could not comprehend what it was; yet, she knew it when she saw it. It was there in their eyes ... in their quacks. It was more than eagerness, delight, or energy; it was something so incomprehensible that, in her mind's eye she could see only darkness.

A duck quacked.

A beam of light pierced the darkness, and she knew it was a place where time did not exist.

"Put that picture clearly in your minds, boys and girls," she said as she told the class about her experience. "A beam of light

21

piercing the darkness where time does not exist." She looked at their blank stares, and continued.

"When I left, I could not get this awesome experience out of my mind: ducks quacking, their eyes gleaming. Ducks. Just ordinary stupid ducks. What's wrong with me? I chalked it up to a mood swing, a state of mind, a little lunacy.

"I went to a grocery store, and almost forgot about my little encounter with the twilight zone, when I saw a young woman who was a known prostitute. As she walked toward me in her mini-skirt, I saw the eyes of other women look away as if she were not there. She reached in front of me to take something off the shelf, and as she was about to put it in her basket, our eyes met.

"There it was again! This time, chills pierced my back. She looked at me confused. I said, hi, and she responded with a pleasant smile. She seemed delighted that someone had given her the simple courtesy of recognition.

"What was it that I saw in the face of a prostitute and the eyes of ducks? I had no idea. Now I was really worried. I must be nuts." Students laughed, but listened intently.

"After that, the sun was brighter, trees were not just trees, and people were more than pathetic human beings.

"Later, for the sake of my own sanity, I tried to put it in words: What I saw was the universal principle, a principle which operates always and everywhere. All things express this principle, even down to the last molecule in the universe.

"When the ducks quacked, they quacked, I AM! As I looked at the prostitute's face, it said ... I AM!

The class had mixed feelings; some students looked at each other as if to say: weird! Others seemed to grasp something no teacher had ever taught before.

Her eyes seemed to sparkle with the light of truth, like the moon reflecting the brilliance of the sun. She continued, undaunted.

"In everything we do, in every word we speak, and in every thought we think, we say, over and over ... I AM!"

"Even hookers?" a voice asked from the back of the room.

Everybody giggled.

"No, Jason, not *even* hookers. When you say even hookers, you set them apart. Even prostitutes say, I am."

Some of the students understood; others had no grasp whatsoever.

Their derision was justified now, and they were convinced more than ever that she was just a kooky lady.

Teachers and parents became more aloof; they felt it was wrong to raise prostitutes up to a level of respect, it had to be stopped.

"You can't teach our children to honor sluts. What's wrong with you?" But Sarah knew that even as they insulted her, they too were saying ... I am. If they wanted to believe she was loony, so be it. What she knew in her heart was so great ... so awesome ... that when she thought about it, her whole body felt limp.

When the school year ended, she returned to full-time family life, never to teach again.

"We teach our kids all wrong," she told the principal. "We need to stop teaching, and get out of the way."

"I'm sorry, Mrs. Figueroa, but we can't have our teachers telling us how to run the system."

But she was in control now. Sarah's secret was real.

She spoke with a calm and dignity unbecoming a person with no credibility as she said, "Who are you?"

"Huh?"

"Alan Watts once said, 'we cannot know *what* to do until we know *who* we are.' No wonder the country is going to hell in a hand-basket ... we haven't been introduced to the ducks." She smiled as she left.

Robert Frauenhofer

Angie's Ghost

*D*on was the only person who understood why Sarah would be content with her commitment to him and the kids; but this I am business did not explain the secret which, apparantly, was over his head. Was that it maybe? Had she deluded herself into believing that she knew something us ordinary people could not comprehend, so she could manintain her all-knowing teacher status? Still, he knew she was right about his feelings of emptiness. He pushed it out of his mind and prepared for a glorious day.

She loved their weekends in San Francisco, and always stopped at the bridge. It was more than the Golden Gate; it was a symbol of their unity. Someday the kids would bring their own children, and remember the good times they'd had.

"But it's just a bridge," Don teased, "steel ... paint."

"It's not just a bridge; it's still the biggest tourist attraction in the world ... ahead of the Eiffel Tower. And the view is awesome, and the fog when it stops against the bridge on the ocean side. It looks like cotton, and the other side is perfectly clear and sunny. Where else can you see that? And life ... most of all ... life!"

"Yeah, I know. You say it every time we get on the bridge: look how lively it is ... whoopee!"

"It's true! San Francisco is a lively town. Happy faces, excitement ... it's all there on the bridge ... just like when Candy bounced off the chair just now. Those people are bouncy. You'll see bikers here, joggers there, tourists from all over the world, ships, sailboats, hang-gliders ..."

"Thieves."

"So what?" She waved her arms excitedly. "We got thieves in congress, universities, churches."

"And city officials who steal thirteen million and stash it just before jumping off your beloved bridge."

"Forget it. We're going on a picnic, and we're stopping at my bridge."

"You and your bridge."

She ignored him. "I could live on the bridge. It's my favorite place in the whole world. When I die, I want my ashes scattered from the bridge. Better still ... keep my body in one piece and drop it over the side. Cover it with shark bait so I can nourish life in the sea."

"We'll drop you naked over the edge."

"Yes."

"In fact, why wait? We could do it today while you're still alive. Sharks like their food fresh."

"Will you quit making fun of me just because I have a thing about the bridge?"

"And ducks."

Her glassy stare told him she hadn't heard that last remark.

Kevin jumped into the doorway. "Are we ready yet?"

"Kevin! After all the trouble you had over that kite, you bring it in here?"

He tried to defend himself, but it was clumsy, and he knew it. "How do you know it's the same one if it's all folded and wrapped up?"

She stared at him.

"OK, I think maybe it is ... it is the same one; but this is different. It's for the Marina this time."

"Didn't your dad tell you to get rid of it?"

Kevin looked at Don who looked at Sarah sheepishly.

"Don, how can he learn if you ... after what he did with that thing."

He spoke in a deep voice as if to maintain his authority. "I'm not defending him. Kevin, put it in the car ... right now."

Like a sling-shot pulled and ready, Kevin had aimed himself from the door in anticipation as they spoke. He was gone before Don finished.

"You see? He knew you'd get him off the hook."

"He was punished; besides, Angie's parents and their ghosts had a part in it. It's their own fault for teaching her that kind of stuff."

"They're entitled to believe what they want. Besides, Kevin knew how she felt and he took advantage of it. Imagine a kid doing a thing like that with a kite. You never should have told him that story about Tibet. You and your stories."

"It was perfectly innocent."

"But you know Kev is hyper', and what he might do with the power of suggestion."

"It's just energy; he's got more than any two people in the world."

She paused, then softened her tone. "Well, we know it wasn't malicious, but others may not understand."

"You mean the kite thing," he said as he looked out the window. Finally, after a long silence, he turned back to her and said, "But you gotta admit, it was good."

Sarah smirked as she thought about it. "Yeah, a chip off the old block."

The infamous kite incident had received more notoriety than it deserved. As a result, Kevin became known as the kite-man, a name he accepted with pride.

Angie Skipper had been a laughing stock. She lived in a big two-story house, an only child of rich parents who believed they had seen a ghost in the hallways. All the kids teased Angie; but she defended her beliefs. She had heard noises and knew there had to be something evil happening in that house. Maybe that explained the scared look on her face.

Don had not known about Angie when he told Kevin about the tradition of kite flying in Tibet: For construction, they used fine silk over bamboo framework. As a source of family honor, it had to be of the finest material and craftsmanship. Often fitted with dragon heads and shards of broken glass, these fine kites could bring down rivals in the annual competition. At night, they would send their kites aloft with little butter-lamps inside and the dragon's eyes would glow red. Shells were attached to produce a wailing sound as the wind swirled.

With sheer delight, Kevin's mind seized upon the thought of building a magnificent kite while providing a service for Angie which she was sure to appreciate. A little imagination and an accomplice were all he needed to put together a great scheme. He was very experienced with kites; he loved to go to the Marina and lift the big ones to the wind with his dad while mom admired her bridge.

After several weeks of building and testing, he finally decided that the perfect time had arrived. On a breezy night, he and his best friend, Cal, walked down a narrow road in Mill Valley. They wore black pants and black turtle neck sweaters so they would not be seen.

"How we gonna fly a kite with all these trees?"

"No problem, the whole back yard is clear. Her bedroom is in a perfect spot upstairs. Now I'm glad I went to her birthday party. You got the pebbles?"

Cal showed him a bulge in his pocket.

Kevin was excited about the little plot he had cooked up, but not sure if it would work. His tests proved he could maneuver the kite; but if the wind was not just right, it might shift or jerk too quickly. He had to hold it still and move it slowly for the best effect.

"Right here. This is it. I'll go first. Stay here until I'm ready."

Cal waited patiently as Kevin climbed over the fence and checked the area.

"OK, hand it over. Careful! Watch the string!"

Cal pushed the kite over and waited as they had planned. He served as a look-out until Kevin was in position across the yard. A short hoot and Cal scaled the fence low and quiet. They felt good ... like GI's.

Lights were still on in the house and they could see shadows move across the curtains. They would wait until Angie went to her Bedroom. Twenty minutes seemed like an hour as Kevin leaned against the house, string in hand, below Angie's bedroom window. Cal stood behind a shrub across the lawn and stared through field glasses into the open window where curtains had not been drawn. The light came on and Cal ran quietly to Kevin's side.

"She's there. Quick, let 'er up."

"Turn on the light first."

Cal clicked on the little flashlight attached to the inside of the kite, and admired Kevin as he skillfully maneuvered it into position.

"Yeah! It's right next to the window. Listen to the shells; it's perfect."

Three shells attached to the kite made a soft whispering howl as the wind blew through them.

"Throw the pebbles, quick."

Cal grabbed from the pea gravel in his pocket and aimed for the window.

"Can't you even hit a window?"

"The shells are makin' enough noise ... it sounds scary. She should hear it through the open window."

Kevin moved the kite slowly up and down to get her attention. She heard the noise and looked up expecting to see a ghost. What she saw was partly in her mind's eye, and partly the face on the kite with a flashlight behind it as the hair on her neck pricked straight up through goose bumps.

"Aghheeeeeeeee!" she screamed. "Aagghhh!" With very little pause to catch her breath, she screamed again, and again, and again.

"Let's get out of here. Pull the kite down. Let go!"

"No." Kevin was determined to bring his kite back intact.

"She won't stop. She thinks it's a real ghost. I'm gone." Cal rocketed to the fence on a squirt of adrenaline, and leaped to the top.

"Wait. I got it. I'm right behind you." Kevin pulled the kite behind him as it leaped up and down like a wild horse unwilling to go back to the barn. "Damn! She's going crazy. Shut up already! Here. I'll hand it over."

"Let it go; it's too windy."

"No. I put too much work into it."

"She finally stopped screamin'," Cal said as he grabbed the string attached to the base of the kite. "Somebody's comin' ... let it go. The wind's got it! I can't hold it down!"

"Yes you can. Pull it!"

Cal finally managed to hold it steady; but the string got caught on the fence.

"Turn off the light so they won't see us."

Too late. Angie's dad had shot out the back door and started across the lawn; but Kevin would not give up on his kite. "My knife, I'll cut it. Just run for it.!"

Cal never ran so fast in his life, while Kevin led his pursuer in a different direction, all part of their contingency plan. He easily escaped Mr. Skipper who was more intent on taking care of his daughter than he was on catching Kevin. He knew who he was, and would deal with him later.

The two adventurers met at a designated spot where Kevin was relieved to see Cal with his kite still in perfect condition.

When he finally returned home, kite in hand, kevin was not surprised to see his mom and dad waiting for him at the front door.

Sarah was the first to speak.

"Oh, God! Let me see that thing." She grabbed it angrily. "Look at this, Don. Just like you described in your stupid stories. Look at this hideous face. I'd be scared myself if I saw this thing float by my window."

Don almost smiled, but he recognized the seriousness of the matter, as Mr. Skipper had clearly and rudely explained on the phone.

"Kevin! You scared the living shit out of her."

"I didn't know she'd go bonkers. I thought ..."

"What did you expect?"

"Well, she always said she heard ghosts. She bragged about it. I figured she wasn't afraid of them. Once she saw the face, she could go back and tell the kids she really saw it. I didn't think ... the way she screamed and screamed ... on and on."

"Of course. She was terrified! And her parents are furious. And so am I."

Don was not very convincing; he knew it would take more than a scolding to get through to him. Kevin was grounded for a month and told to get rid of the kite. That was easy ... plenty of space over the ceiling in the garage. He always found a way to get around what he thought were unreasonable demands.

How was he to know Angie would take it so hard. She wanted her ghost to be real; and he gave her what she wanted. He wasn't happy about the punishment; but something inside felt good knowing that he had pulled it off. They would laugh about it later after things cooled down. Besides, dad would be proud when he saw it flying in San Francisco; everybody would admire his fine kite.

Angie's mother had contained her anger as she spoke calmly but prophetically to Sarah: "Someday, that boy's attitude will get him in very serious trouble."

Trouble came easy to Kevin, even when he wasn't looking for it; but this time, he had given it a little assist.

As the family drove toward San Francisco in the brand new red van with a picnic lunch and high hopes for a fun day, they were aware of the risk; but they would not be intimidated by greedy stalkers.

Sarah was prepared with mace in her purse, but did not realize that Kevin had packed something else. Hidden in the middle of the kite was a forbidden water pistol; it was so realistic, it could be mistaken for the real thing. In Kevin's mind, it might be useful to bluff attackers; he never thought it could mean the difference between life and death.

Robert Frauenhofer

The Fall

*T*he Golden Gate Bridge!

Why were so many people attracted to it? What was the mystery of this place?

It was more than esthetics, the view, the construction, or the history; it was the human spirit! To build it had taken determination, perseverance, persuasion, vision.

Men had struggled with the elements, and risked their lives. Their spirit was in every cable, every rivet. The sounds of the bridge were their sounds; the fog was their touch.

There were some who could pass over this mighty bridge, and think it was just concrete, steel and paint; but for those who admired it, it was much more. As they gazed at its awesome lines against the sky, what they really admired was the human soul.

It was not just another bridge built with sweat and blood; it was an entity, and it was born on a glorious day in May, 1937 to the delight of two hundred thousand people who turned out for its delivery.

America would never be the same; it was a new land. Once again we had broken the bonds of common sense, and had reached a new area of possibility.

When a man dreams a dream, when his vision is clear and powerful, and when the emotion he attaches to it is so strong that he cannot let go of it even if it means his own death, then his dream will be realized.

His dream will be realized!

There it was ... shining, gleaming, glistening, humming. There it was in all its glory, and it said ... I AM!

The first day was pedestrian day; you could walk across one-way for a nickel, and a nickel back. People ran, jumped, roller-skated, stilt-walked and danced across their newly born infant. They spread their picnics in the middle of the road, bought thousands of hot dogs, took pictures, whistled, sang, laughed, admired.

What they experienced out there was not just another world, it was another dimension. The next day when cars were allowed to cross for the first time, they came from as far away as Canada and Alaska. From both sides of the bridge, horns blared, church bells rang, and people cheered as police cars and fire trucks led the way with sirens shrieking. Foghorns bellowed, bells clanged, and whistles blew from ocean liners, tugboats, freighters, and navy ships.

The celebration lasted for a week. It included torchlight parades, lavish balls, concerts, fireworks, dancing and singing in the streets, and even the New Year's ceremonial dragon dancing through the streets of Chinatown.

From that day on, the bridge has always been a place where life, vitality and energy abound.

Herbert Nash displayed his share of energy as he walked menacingly through the trees toward the bridge. Joggers and bikers hurried their pace at the sight of this ugly human being; his face was blotched, warted and hideous, his nose almost flat. At six-feet-four, his two-hundred-sixty pound frame was all muscle ... no fat. Lifting weights and building muscle were his way of telling people not to mess with him.

He was much too sensitive to criticism, and never seemed to know for sure if people were just joking good-naturedly or maliciously poking fun. To him, all razzing was mean-spirited ridicule. Why do people have to be like that?

His emotional instability caused a form of pain no one else could understand ... no one except Sean, his best and only friend. Herbert was easily led, even now at the age of forty-one; Sean, two years his senior, took advantage of this and manipulated him for his own ends.

An acquaintance at Sid's Bar in Potrero once called him Herbert the pervert, and ended up in the hospital; but the charges were dropped when Sean "persuaded" the victim to be nice.

'After all, Herbert had emotional problems; besides, it could lead to a very volatile situation for all those concerned.' Everyone who knew Sean understood the meaning of those words.

When he was a boy, he used to burn animals alive. He would trap a cat in a cage, and light a small welding torch nearby so the cat would see it and be frightened. Then he would wave the flame at the cat inflicting burns; the cat would jump around the cage in a panic. Finally, after he'd had his "fun", he would squirt lighter fluid and light 'im up.

It was common knowledge that he had also torched people; but there was no proof, he always had an alibi.

A volatile situation for all concerned could only mean members of your family would be put to the torch. Sean enjoyed speaking in his own weird, cryptic language; but, no matter how he said it, everyone knew one thing: he did not bluff ... ever.

Word on the street was that he couldn't get it off unless he watched somebody screaming in pain. Herbert the pervert helped him, and himself, with their sexual needs; but it was too mechanical. When Sean needed a greater thrill, they would go on the prowl for another victim: preferably a transient in another city.

Don and Sarah had not been aware of their reputation when they were threatened by the pair. Had the mob goons not intervened, their lives and their children would have been threatened.

Sean's ambition was to start his own religion and be admired by his followers. His mother had always told him he would someday be a great man remembered in the history books; but he was very mischievous when he was a child, and she feared for his soul. She had to protect this potential world leader from the degradation of modern society.

On a hot summer day, when he was nine years old, an incident occurred which put a new warp on his already twisted mind: Connie, a twelve year-old girl who lived next door, had heard him talking to his dog. She climbed the six foot high wood fence and laughed as she looked down at him. He looked up in surprise as her short, loosely fit dress slid up to her waist and revealed bikini panties which covered very little.

"Help me down ... I'm stuck."

Sean was glad to oblige. With his face touching the back of her legs, he reached for her waist to help her down.

"No ... I'm caught. Push me up a little first. Not like that ... that hurts. Push up from underneath."

He hesitated, then put his hand under her crotch. "Right here?"

"Yes. Push up."

He pushed her up while she pushed away from the fence. He let her down, and felt everything she wanted him to feel.

"I love your little Cockerspaniel," she said innocently. "I heard him digging behind the tool shed yesterday."

"Digging?"

"Yeah. I wonder what he found."

"Maybe a bone."

"Let's go see."

As they walked behind the shed, she pretended to trip on a board, and grabbed him by the arm pulling him down on top of her. Her eyes were inches away from his.

"Are you gonna kiss me?"

His heart was beating fast, and he didn't know what to say. He had always admired Connie from a distance; but they seldom said more than hi to each other. When he talked to her, his mother always seemed to pop up and find something for him to do.

He dry swallowed. "OK."

With his body suspended over hers at arms length, he kissed her with his eyes wide open. She immediately tore his shirt open and worked her hands into his pants; but their little adventure did not last long. Sean's mother had looked out the kitchen window, just as they walked behind the shed. She had always believed the worst about Connie's reputation; and she wasn't about to let her involve Sean in her fantasies. She ran out the door, and rushed around the corner of the shed, standing directly over them. Her eyes bulged uncontrollably; she screamed like a frightened psychopath.

"Yaaagh! You slut!"

Sean instantly leaped straight up, just as she grabbed him by the collar and pulled. It appeared as if she had lifted him with super strength.

Connie almost flew over the fence before she could say another word.

"Get out of here! Begone Satan!"

Sean always felt mildly ashamed in the presence of his mother; but this time he could not look her in the eye.

She pulled him into the house with an iron grip on his wrist. She was so agitated, she had to wait to catch her breath. Finally, she spoke with great emotion.

"If a man so much as looks after a woman, it is better to pluck out his eyes than to endure hell and damnation forever and ever!"

She turned on an electric burner on the stove while she held his wrist.

"See how hot that is? Put your hand near it!" She held him close enough to feel the heat; it was red hot.

"Ma! No! Maaa!"

"I want you to know that's nothing compared to the pain of hell, and it goes on forever! Forever and ever! You can never escape!"

"No! No! Please, MA!"

"I don't want to do this ... I ... I don't want you to suffer."

His voice quivered as he said, "I'll never do anything wrong again. I promise! No!"

He cried as his hand got hotter, and he pulled against her strength. "Don't resist! You'll thank me. Do you think I would let my boy suffer in hell? Do you think I would let Satan win this battle? I will show him. You will be great! This is your test!"

"No. Please ma. No. Aaaagh!"

37

Suddenly, she plunged his hand into the burner; he fainted at the smell of his own flesh burning. When he came to, she was crying, and treating his burned hand. The pain was unbearable.

There is a special relationship between mother and son; but when bonding occurs in a strange way, as it had for Sean, it's impossible to become anything more than an extension of the mother. The burning of his hand was a traumatic experience which shaped his mind in her image forever.

He could not blame her; nor could he blame himself, since he was her son. His twisted, confused mind would spin a web of rationalization to make it all right.

When he preached to Herbert, he sounded like a man trying to convince himself of something. Herbert easily agreed with everything he said. It was not they who burned people alive; it was Agni, the fire god, who worked through them ... Agni, consumer of flesh given in sacrifice.

"You see, Herbert how clear it is? Even scientists know it was lightning! Ha, ha, ha." His enthusiasm turned to hysteria. "Lightning, the spark that energized gases and formed carbon molecules. Of course! Carbon molecules, the soup of life. All life evolved from there. But we know where the lightning came from, don't we?"

Herbert would stare into his eyes, and shake his head obediently. It was almost comical to see this small, pale man manipulate a powerhouse like Herbert.

"Agni was the true spark which gave life to man. He was born in heaven as flames of the sun, and descended to earth in the shape of lightning. And when he returns, he will consume the earth by fire. Destruction is always necessary for renewal." He smiled and straightened his poor posture as he said, "Death is necessary before new life can form. Death."

"Yes."

"We must build a church! We must honor Agni!"

"Yes."

"And they will understand my power when the bomb blows. Just a small bomb for starters, but a humble beginning will lead to bigger things. The money comes first. Thirteen million would really get us started. Between that and my faithful Sparks, we will build a powerful organization."

As he walked toward the bridge, Herbert thought about the couple in Mill Valley. He didn't believe they had the money. If they didn't, it was still here somewhere between the bridge and Baker Beach.

Herbert's eyes widened as he thought about it. "Thirteen million ... the gods will lead us."

His job was to stay here in the area as much as possible and look for clues. Like a faithful soldier, he would walk the grounds from Zack's house to Fort Point every day watching, searching. He wore Levi's, running shoes, dark glasses and always a back-pack. He knew the undercover people had watched his every move, and he knew who they were. But today they were gone, at last ... gave up ... convinced that Zack's pursuers had caught up with him, and had taken the money.

Certainly, the mob didn't have it, because they were keeping a close watch on the couple in Mill Valley; and after their little skirmish this morning, Sean too was convinced Don and Sarah didn't have it.

As he walked down the hill to Fort Point, Herbert remembered it was Saturday ... tourists everywhere. He thought about the many times he had toured the fort and walked the roof where cannons would have defended the channel against invaders. The roof was the first place the police had searched; and it was only logical that the money could have fallen from the bridge above.

He knew the money was not there; but he also knew it had not been found anywhere in the area. He had been there night and day, and knew all the best surveillance points.

"Give it up; it ain't here," a white-haired old man said to Herbert's back as he pushed his cane into his neck.

"Uh, hi. Didn't see ya there. You cut your beard again."

"I like to keep it cut sharp ... makes my face look chiseled ... covers up my double chin. Shave this thing off, and I look like a frog. Why do you think most guys wear a beard? They hide behind it. Why don't you do that? You hide behind those big dark glasses, why not a beard?"

"Why don't you mind your own business, ol' man?"

"Why don't you wise up and take my advice? If I was as ugly as you, I'd be wearin' more than a beard. And one more piece of advice ... I been walkin' this place for thirty years, and I can tell ya there ain't no suitcase fulla money sittin' around here. Ain't no suitcase big enough to hold thirteen million, either."

"You told me that yesterday and the day before; but Sean says there's ... a thousand acres where it could be. It's here ... an' it's mine ... me and Sean. We earned it. I put my time in this place."

The old man looked at him with pity. "You're barkin' up the wrong tree ... you and this Sean guy. The goons got some of it when they killed him on the bridge ... chopped his hand off to get it ... but the rest is gone forever."

"Yeah? You been talkin' to too many squirrels."

"You may be right, but those critters got more sense than you do; at least they know where to go for food."

"Big deal. You show off in front of tourists by makin' squirrels crawl up your leg for nuts. So what?"

As thin-skinned as Herbert was, he could argue incessantly with this old man and never get offended. It wasn't what the old guy said, but how he said it. Even as his words indicated disrespect, something about him seemed to give complete acceptance. It was something which Herbert rarely experienced.

How could he have friends with a face like that? Women walking behind him admired his physique; but when they saw his face, they were surprised, and could not hide their reaction.

Then there were the ones who tried to pretend they didn't care. They would talk to him as if he were no different than anybody else; but they were disingenuine, and he knew it.

At least the old man was honest ... told it like it was. If anybody else had said those things to him, he'd be dead ... worse than dead. Once Herbert lost control, he was unstoppable.

Crazy old guy ... but he liked Herbert, and it wasn't pity; it was genuine respect. Even Sean did not respect him like this. Sean accepted him as his best friend; but only on Sean's terms.

"Well, I hope you trip over the money, and break a leg.

"Uh ... see ya ... ol' man."

The old man had just wished him well in a language Herbert understood. The words had not been direct, but they went directly to the heart. In a crazy world where children receive no love and affection, direct words of praise, acceptance and respect do not work.

As he limped away, Herbert spoke clumsily. "I hope you ... trip on yer cane."

The place was packed with tourists ... no point in staying here. He decided to walk up to vista point above the fort near the toll gates. As many times as he'd been there, he still enjoyed the view.

A bright red van pulled up to a parking meter where the family of four excitedly prepared for a romp on the bridge. Herbert recognized Sarah and quickly looked away so she would not see his face. Candy was excited because her mother was excited. "Let's go ma! Last one on the bridge is a soft-boiled egg."

"Hard ... I mean ... rotten egg." Kevin responded.

"You sure it's not scrambled?" Don joked.

"Now you're talking about her brain."

Sarah scolded Kevin without looking back. "Kevin, be nice."

Herbert was impressed by her beauty, and wanted to look back at her as he listened to their conversation. How great it must be to belong to a family like that. He had never had that experience. He had been raised by a mother who didn't want him; she abandoned him when he was eight years old.

Abandonment is the worst thing you can do to a child. He wished he had been beaten, abused, starved ... anything but abandoned. Never to have felt her warm embrace, never to have been wanted, the feeling of emptiness ... nothingness.

Yet, something in him had fought back; he had survived on the streets. Sean had taken him in when he was nineteen, and had given him a reason to live: to build a church.

Candy ran toward the bridge. "Come on, mom!"

Sarah started, then turned back to look at the big man who had turned to look at her. When their eyes met, she recognized him as the man with the flat nose who had confronted them earlier. 'He wouldn't try anything here,' she thought. 'He must be here to keep an eye on us. Must have followed us.'

He wondered why they had returned to the bridge. She turned and walked quickly as his eyes followed, her leotards revealed a figure that turned him into a ballistic missile. He wanted to follow her, but he realized how bad he would look with this bulge in his pants; people stared at him enough as it was. He leaned on the fence, and tried to get his mind off of this beautiful lady who could never be part of his life.

"Dad. Let's go!"

"Go ahead, Kev. I'm gonna fix this seat; it sticks."

Herbert glanced at the red van, and then stared back at the bridge where Sarah and Candy walked. They were getting close to the area of the "jump" where Zack Pinches had gone over. He could hear the conversation between father and son as Kevin stalled.

"What are you doing, Kevin? Close the door."

"OK. I just wanted to get some ... gum, see?"

"Tell mom I'll catch up."

Kevin ran for the bridge holding one hand in front of him, so Don could not see the water pistol which he had taken from under the seat. As he passed, Herbert caught a glimpse of the gun, and was sure it was real. He assumed he hid it from his dad so he could protect himself from potential kidnappers who thought they had the money.

Sarah and Candy jogged happily toward the center of the bridge as Kevin approached the "jump" scene where a fat lady talked excitedly to her daughter. She pointed to a sea gull

42

perched on the railing at exactly the spot where Zack had jumped.

"Look at the sea gull! He's so close!"

"He's not even afraid, mom."

Kevin could not resist ... what a shot. He immediately pointed the gun at the bird, and pulled the trigger; but the wind curved the water into the lady's face just as she turned toward him.

She was a tourist from a small town in Ohio, and had been warned about the crime in San Francisco, and the mystery surrounding the bridge.

For an instant, she thought the gun was real.

"Yaagghh!" She gasped for air as if she were having an attack. Then, as she clutched her throat, she fell to the pavement and lost consciousness.

Her daughter screamed for help as tourists gathered around, and Kevin backed up to the rail in disbelief. He didn't realize that he was still pointing the gun at the lady, even as she lay motionless on the ground.

A man pointed to kevin and yelled, "He did it! I saw him!"

"Get him, quick!"

"No! It's not a real gun!" Kevin screamed.

Tourists swarmed on him thinking he had shot the lady. Suddenly, he was on the railing, holding onto a vertical cable as he kicked at the people.

"No! Get down!"

The bay, two-hundred feet below, seemed to have arms which reached up and pulled.

"Give me the gun!"

"Ahhhhhhh!"

People screamed and fainted as Kevin fell into the bay. A man watched as Kevin went in feet first. He knew that the powerful undercurrents could sweep a body out to sea very quickly.

43

Herbert saw the fall from his position near the parking lot. He immediately turned toward Don who looked at him, startled. His stare told Don something bad had happened.

"What? What happened?!"

Herbert could not talk.

Don yelled for Kevin as he ran for the bridge.

"Where are you? Kevin! Will you people get out of my way!"

Horns blasted as he ran in the road toward the scene where a crowd gathered.

"What happened?"

"She's dead."

"What?"

"The boy ... he ..."

"What! Where? Where is he?"

"Gone," a man said, his voice cracking. "He's gone."

Sarah and Candy ran to the scene to see what had happened.

"Dad!"

"Oh my God! No!"

Don ran to the rail and looked down.

"Dad!"

Sarah froze.

He jumped into the road, and raced through oncoming traffic to get off the bridge as fast as possible. In trying to avoid him, cars slammed into each other, and created a traffic jam that would reach for miles into San Francisco.

Herbert chased after him when he saw him scramble down the hill in a panic.

"No! I have to save my boy! You're ... you're ..."

Herbert tackled him just as he reached the water's edge. A huge wave slammed against the rocks, and pulled them toward the sea; but Herbert called on every ounce of strength to drag himself and Don back. After a wild struggle, Don realized that, even with adrenaline pumping, he was no match for this big man. He cried as Herb held him down, and tourists tried to figure out what had happened.

"Sarah! I need to get back! Let me up!"

Herbert released him and watched with amazement as Don bounded up the hill like a mountain goat. He grabbed onto shrubs and pulled himself along without concern for the cuts and bruises on his face.

It was pandemonium on the bridge. As police arrived, rumors spread quickly: another jump had taken place at exactly the same spot where Zack went over. A strong voice above the noise of the crowd seemed to take on the responsibility to inform everybody of the latest theory: "The kid had the money ... and he was armed!"

A lady responded with her own conclusion. "He must have taken it with him when he fell off the bridge."

Don worked his way through the crowd until he found Sarah with Candy crying in her arms.

The crowd turned vicious. "It's their fault! They're the ones ... the couple on TV. They came back for the money."

A woman turned her eyebrows down in a show of disdain and screamed, "You sent your own son to his death so you could get the money! You scum!"

"We should throw you over with him, you miserable bastards!"

A teenager chimed in, "How could you? You give your own boy a gun and tell him to do your dirty work. People like you should be ..."

Sarah ignored them and comforted Candy. "It's OK. It's all right."

Don could not believe how calm she was.

"It's OK, Don. It's OK."

"What! He's gone ... Kevin ..." Anguish tore his face apart.

"No. He's alive ... I ... know it."

Don looked at her in total confusion as she held Candy by the arm pits.

"Look at me. See? I'm not even crying ... because I know ... I know he's alive. I know we'll get him back."

45

Don tried to believe her, but the shock was too much. He screamed as police approached. "Save my boy! Save him!"

He ran back to the railing, and looked down. In his confused mind, he thought he could jump into the bay and save Kevin. A hand gripped his shoulder as if to say, 'don't do it'.

"I'm sorry, sir. The Coast Guard has been notified. Helicopters are on the way. Are you all right, ma'am?"

"Yes. The lady. She ..."

Sarah pointed to the dead woman and her daughter. She took the girl in her arms to comfort her.

Death was here in this place; she felt it in the deepest part of her soul. Something out there, something beyond comprehension, seemed to touch this spot as if it were feeling its way into our world. Yet, she did not fear for Kevin's safety.

She felt as if she were standing over her shoulder looking down at herself; she was the observer and the observed.

At a time when she should have been concerned only with her own grief, she cared for this girl who had lost her mother.

For an instant, she wondered about her own sanity. Maybe the teachers were right: maybe she really was loony.

Don was out of his mind. "I'm goin' after my boy! He might be on the beach, or in the rocks!"

"There's nothing you can do, sir. let the Coast Guard handle it."

"No. I'm going!"

Sarah and Candy ran after Don as he rammed his way through the crowd.

"Sir, I need a report."

"Watch it!"

"Damn! The guy's knockin' people over like bowling pins. Where does he think he's going?"

"Won't do any good. It's useless. The body's headin' out to sea by now."

But Don would not give up. He drove down to Baker Beach and searched, while helicopters flew low along the coast. Candy stayed in the van to listen to a local radio station in case they got a report.

"Keviiinnnn! Keviiinnnn!" Don ran along the beach while sun-bathers watched curiously.

"I wonder if they're making a movie," a teen girl said as she looked for a camera in the helicopter.

"Well, if they are, the guy's a good actor."

Sarah stood motionless on the beach as Candy sat in the van.

"Mom!" Candy called as she poked her head out the window.

" They're talking about it now."

Sarah leaned against the van to listen as the announcer continued: "Another tragedy at the exact same spot on the bridge where Zack went over. This time, a boy ... we don't know the age ... no name; but it has been confirmed by witnesses at the scene. Mac?"

"Yes, John. I'm here."

"Let's go to the bridge for the latest report. From the Golden Gate Bridge for KPO, here's Mac Rogers."

"Yes, John, it was the son ... the couple from Mill Valley who said they were trying to save the homeless guy ... an alleged member of the suicide cult, the Sparks. Remember them? They were accused of having the money?"

"Yes, Mac. What were they doing there?"

"Witnesses here say they were trying to retrieve it from the outside of the bridge, just under a steel bar. Apparently, it was wedged into the bridge where it was not visible. It would have been just a matter of time before the crews out here found it. This is the exact spot where Zack's hand was found and where the Spark jumped.

"I have a man here ... sir ... would you tell us exactly what you saw?"

"I ... that kid ... that poor kid ... I'll never forget the look on his face when he went ... I ... can't."

"That's OK, I understand," Mac said as the man walked away. "It's OK ... to cry."

"John ... the people here are grief stricken. I'll do the best I can. They say the boy was searching for the money through the girders ... couldn't reach it ... decided to climb the rail, and get it from a position outside the bridge. People grabbed at him to stop what they thought was a suicide attempt ... he fell. Several people said they saw something else fall with him ... it could only have been the money ... thirteen million ... doesn't seem possible.

"According to the Coast Guard, the body could end up in Monterey, if it's ever found at all.

"But he was armed. Can you believe it? The boy was armed. The people believe the parents were responsible. They were ready to tear those people apart. An investigation is sure to follow ... there may be an arrest."

Sarah was shocked. "What! My boy is gone and they ... no. No body will be found because there is no body ... he's alive! I'm his mother, and I would feel his death."

Don would not argue with her. She needed time to get over the shock; perhaps this was how her mind coped until she had a chance to digest it. He thought about the possibility that she might be right; but he would continue the search.

He scrambled back into the van.

"We're goin' down the coast ... Cliff House ... beach ... rocks."

Sarah acquiesced. As he approached the Cliff House at high speed, tourists scattered and jumped from the cross-walk. When he reached Ocean Beach, he screeched to a halt, and ran out to the water's edge.

How could a twelve year-old boy survive a fall like that? Where would he be if he did?

A dense fog moved slowly toward the Golden Gate Bridge; Don stared at it in despair. Normally, he would have marveled at the sight. It really did look like cotton ... the way Kevin used to describe it.

Finally, when he walked back to the van, Sarah said, "I know you doubt me, Don. I don't blame you; I have no explanation. I only know ... death has not arrived in this family. I know it. I want to go back to the bridge. He's not here."

Don was bewildered. He had lost his son; there was no hope. If she wanted to go back to her bridge ... well, maybe it would comfort her.

His body went through the motions: put it in gear, stomped on it, fought the traffic; but he didn't feel anything, didn't see anything, didn't hear anything.

Everything was illusion. Wherever Kevin was, that was reality ... that's where Don was.

"Candy, just lie down and rest."

"But, daddy's driving so fast."

"Don, slow down."

"I can't believe this is happening. Why? What was he doing there? Why did that lady die on the bridge? What's going on here? How could he have seen the money? He was so hyper ... he used to ..."

"He *is* hyper. I told you ... he's alive."

"We should go back to the beach. We have another hour of daylight. We have another hour of daylight. We ... have ..."

"No. Go back to the bridge."

"The bridge. That's all I hear. The bridge. You'd think it was alive. It's just steel ... paint. Ever since that Spark jumped our whole life ... I'm so confused right now."

Sarah stared straight ahead. "Go back," she said with determination.

He snapped out of it. He knew her mind was made up; and it didn't matter, anyway. What good would it do to run up and down the beaches screaming at the ocean. Might as well go back, and sit in the van ... mourn.

As he passed the Cliff House, he recalled the good times Kevin had had in this area, always taking chances against the dangers of the cliffs and the treacherous waves. They had walked through the cave carved out for the old Sutro Baths. His body could be there on the other side caught in the jagged rocks.

49

In an effort to avoid despair, Don grabbed for straws: "Do you believe that stuff about floaters?"

"I ... felt something out there. It's hard to explain ... like an out-of-body experience. I was almost floating above myself, looking down."

"Yes, but ... floaters claim they literally floated in the air ... and always above that spot. That spot, where Kevin fell, the lady died, Zack Pinches ..."

"Kevin is alive."

"I never finished the story he wanted me to finish ... the secret."

"What secret?"

"The secret of life."

"Tell it to him next time you see him."

Don drove slowly and in silence. Finally, he looked at her, and said, "I will."

The Winner

*J*im King, a 22 year-old college student, decided to try his luck one more time before driving back to the Bay Area. As he pulled into the parking lot of the last casino before stateline, he couldn't help thinking about the mystery in San Francisco, and considered stopping on the bridge on the way home. He was too honest to take the money if he found it, but his anger made him think about the possibility.

His peers called him square-face, block-head, and Frankenstein. Yet, he was handsome in his own way in spite of his squareness. He tried to tell himself he didn't care, but their laughter swirled in his head. Why must they ridicule everything?

Wouldn't they be surprised if he actually found thirteen million bucks. Now, as he walked toward the casino, he was pulled between his honesty and his desire for money, money he could use to show them. It was painful to be a laughing stock, but it was more painful to go against his honest nature.

Cold air descended from the Sierras as wind blew fiercely through the foothills toward Reno and the desert below. Tourists ran for the casino to take cover while Jim stood, enchanted by the sound of the wind, his hair blowing wildly in all directions.

Something was in these winds, something mysterious, he could feel it. The Indians knew these winds; they carried with them mysteries of the past. If you listened, you could hear voices from long ago, voices of children playing ... cries of animals dying. You could smell fires burning ... fires whose ashes no longer existed. To the east, Reno was not an anachronism, but a culmination of those mysteries. Reno's children still played, her animals died, and her fires produced the sweet smells of a feast without end.

He entered the casino still preoccupied with his anger, his wind blown hair pointing straight out from the temples. While his square shoulders, dilated eyes and stiff, hesitant walk

51

produced a monster image, his height, five-eight, would not scare anyone. He was such a spectacle that even the most fanatical gamblers took their attention away from their games and stared at him. Dealers dropped cards, heads turned, handles pulled slowly as everyone witnessed his strange entrance. Security guards touched their weapons as if prepared for a crazed killer; but Jim's expression told them not to worry.

There was something in his face so powerful and so intense, it caused people to do a double-take and stare in confusion.

"Watch where you're going," a man said as he stepped aside. "You stupid ..." He looked at Jim's face and stopped like a hummingbird in mid flight; but Jim was not even aware of his presence as he left him choking on words unspoken.

"I'll show 'em," Jim babbled as he looked back at the glass doors he had just entered. Eyes looked toward the door in anticipation; the sound of the wind became a fiendish howl.

"He's just shit-faced," a man said as he turned back to his machine and pulled the handle. Everybody resumed their gambling as if he had never entered.

He walked aimlessly toward the sound of silver dollars gushing into a machine. A bell rang and a young woman screamed, "Yeeaah! One thousand!"

She scooped coins into a large paper cup as he walked by her unaware of her presence or her good fortune.

He bumped into her knocking the cup out of her hand; silver dollars hit the floor with a splash. People watched curiously as he slowly came out of his trance.

"Oh, my God! Look what you did. You ... you ..."

"I'm sorry," Jim apologized. "Let me do it." He scooped down and crawled through the aisle to retrieve the coins placing them in the cup as the young woman helped.

She turned back to her machine, confused, and pulled the handle. The bell stopped ringing as a man came to pay off the jackpot.

"Your jackpot," he said. "You had a jackpot?"

"Yes. One thousand dollars."

"But you played it off." She breathed heavily as he repeated, "you played it off, lady."

"Lady! My name's Jenny ... Jennifer. Nobody ever called me lady!"

"Sorry, lady ... I can't pay. You don't pull the handle until I've had a chance to call it in. It's the rules."

"But ... I ... I just turned twenty-one, born in 1999," she said breathing harder. The man looked at her with pity as she babbled, "I'm from Colorado ... this is my first time in a casino ... my first time in Nevada ..."

"Don't matter if it's your first time in the world ... or what your name is. You played it off ... I can't pay."

He walked away as she stared at the back of his head.

"Poor thing," an old lady said to a man next to her.

"Yeah," he replied forcefully so everyone could hear. "It was that clod on the floor. He should give her the thousand bucks."

All eyes turned toward Jim who seemed to be in another world as he crawled on hands and knees. He peered under a machine with his face close to the floor, and his ass straight up. Jenny pulled her foot back ready to kick, but resisted the temptation to satisfy her anger.

"Do it! Go ahead, honey."

"No," she said with a grind of her teeth. Then, suddenly, she kicked him as hard as she could. He fell face down on the carpet spilling the coins all over again.

"Look what you made me do! You drunken ... stupid ... yaaaah!" She kicked him again as he tried to get up.

"Yeah. Give it to him!" The crowd cheered her on. She readied her foot again as Jim sat up on the carpet and held his hands out to defend himself.

"I should kick you right in the ... you drunk."

"You don't understand. I'm not drunk. I was just ..."

She looked at his face, and frowned in confusion. It startled her ... he was not drunk or doped up. For the first time, she looked directly into his eyes and was deeply impressed by his handsome features. She glanced at his freakishly square jaw, as everyone did when they first met him ... he was used to it ... but then she stared into his eyes again, and her expression changed to a look of approval.

"Uh ... forget it."

She got down to help with the coins until her long brown hair fell over her eyes and her breasts bulged from her low cut blouse.

"Damn ... I know I could find the money," he said in a hushed voice.

"Find it. It's right here in front of you."

"No. The money."

"What are you talking about? You really are drunk."

"I'm not ... I'm talking about thirteen ..."

"Thirteen what? Are you all right? Don't crawl out there! Oh ..."

Jim was about to pick up a silver dollar when a large shoe covered the coin. He looked up to see a security guard standing with arms folded and looking down disdainfully. He immediately recalled stories he'd heard about drunks who got beat up by security guards. They say transients and known pick-pockets get escorted to the back room where they are thoroughly pounded; and here he was crawling for money, upsetting customers. He got up quickly, and stood straight to show he was no drunk.

"It's OK," Jenny intervened. "He's with me. Just had a few too many."

She was angry, but she liked him. There was something about him ... his face ... it wasn't a mask that covered other faces; it was the only face he had. Whatever he felt right now, there it was in his face. He wasn't here to play poker, that's for sure; he'd go home naked. Yet, she had a feeling ... he was a winner.

The security guard reached down, picked up the coin, and pushed it into Jim's hand as he looked into his glassy eyes suspiciously. Jim looked at the coin in his palm as if he were hypnotized. It was a shiny new coin, and it seemed to generate its own energy as it glistened. For a moment his mind shifted to the wind outside; he started to lose focus, but jenny brought him back.

"Oh, John," she said, "maybe that's your lucky coin. Put it in that machine right there."

"Huh? Oh, yeah." Jim held the coin up in front of the security guard's glaring eyes. "Lucky dollar. I'm ... playing the machines ... see?"

He backed up to the machine, put the coin in the slot, pulled the handle, and looked innocently at the guard, who seemed to know that his name was not John, and he was not with the young lady. He watched the cherries and lemons whiz past the little windows until the guard lost interest, and walked away.

The figure of a genie stopped in the first window, but Jim looked toward the door with no interest in the machine.

"Hey!" Jenny pulled his arm to get his attention as another genie came up in the second window. "Check that."

"What?" Jim said, disoriented. "Check what?"

"Those little guys ... oh ... another one!"

"Oh ..." He glanced at the figures. He knew one more would be a jackpot, but the odds were stacked against it. Four genies? Never happen. His mind wandered again; he saw a blur with colors swirling around.

Then, suddenly, he focused on the genies; they seemed big, clear ... real. The machine slowed ... a genie slid by the fourth window and bounced back.

Click.

"Oh, ooh!" Jenny put her hand over her heart. "Just missed."

"It's always that way. The odds are against it." With palms flattened against the air, he raised his arms in a gesture of futility.

"How much would you have won?"

"It's a progressive jackpot."

She looked at him and waited as if he owed her an explanation; but Jim's mind was working very slowly. Finally, she asked, "What does that mean?"

He took a moment to realize that she had never been in a casino before, then replied, "See those numbers up over your head? Every time you play without hitting the big one, they go up."

"You mean ... four-four-one-one-zero?"

"That's what you would win if you hit it right now."

"Forty-four thousand, one hundred-ten ... dollars?

"Right," Jim said apathetically. "Hey, thanks for helping me out. But my name is Jim, not John."

"Oh, hi John," she said without turning her eyes from the machine. "But ... we just barely missed."

He looked at the machine, then back at her bright hopeful face. "Why are you staring at the genies? Don't expect them to come up ... it's sucker bait. Stick to the machine you're playing. I'll pay you the one thousand you lost. It was my fault."

"Forget that. But look ... look at that guy ... the last one. He's right there. If he just landed there ... one spot away ..." She touched the windows on the machine, and spoke like a child talking to Santa Claus.

Jim knew better. You could play all day and never hit four genies. It's always close; first it misses on the right, then on the left. The jackpot gets higher and higher, and you know it could be the next pull. You're hooked.

"Take my advice: forget it."

But Jenny was excited; she couldn't forget it. She could be on a lucky streak. After all, she had missed out on a one thousand dollar jackpot; then she just missed the fourth genie. That's two close ones. Third time around had to be the one.

"What are you ... an old hand?" she ridiculed. "You don't look old enough to be in this place."

"I'm twenty-two."

"Whoopee! Big shot. High-roller."

He knew better than to argue with her. Better to split. "Look, I'm headed for San Francisco ..."

"No you don't. You owe me. You're gonna help me hit that jackpot."

"What? Not a chance!"

"Then hand over the grand you made me lose."

"I ... could get it. You'd have to trust me."

"No need to. You're a winner. I can feel it."

"Huh? You don't even know me. And after I ... and you kicked me ... and, now I'm a winner?"

"Look, let me buy you a cup of coffee."

"Coffee?" Jim was stunned. The whole thing was crazy. He made her lose a thousand dollars; why should she want to have anything to do with him? "How do you know I wouldn't like a drink?"

"You're a coffee man. I can tell. The snack bar's right there. Fix your hair, John, you're a mess."

"Jim, not John. Jim King." He pushed his hair back. "You sound like my mother. You don't even know me."

"You already said that. So let's talk and then I'll know you, King Jim."

"You sure are ..."

"Presumptuous?"

"But I could be a serial killer for all you know."

"Yeah, right." She smiled as they sat on stools at the snack bar. "People always say I'm too open with strangers. Someday it might catch up with me; be careful, and all that. I guess I was just born that way. Why do we all have to be strangers anyway? Like that guy ... did you hear what he called me? Lady! Hey, lady! Can you beat that? I'm not a lady."

"You're not a lady?"

"Hell, no. I'm Jenny." She pounded her breasts with an open hand. "I'm Jenny! Me! Jenny!"

He watched her breasts heave with each slap of her hand, then looked embarrassed as she caught the gleam in his eye.

"Do you like my boobs?" she asked as the waitress poured coffee and smiled. "I hope I don't embarrass you."

"Around here, nobody cares. But I can't believe you're from Colorado. Aren't they conservative back there?"

"Conservative and up-tight."

"But, I've been there and I found the people very friendly."

"That's because you don't know them."

"You just popped my bubble."

"Well, it's not the whole state. It's just that in some areas, you have to belong to their church and think like they do or you're out."

"I feel rejection here. Are you bitter?"

She wondered if it was a mistake to be so open with him, but continued anyway. "Why can't people respect each other? Why do we have to be strangers? Strangers! What are we, aliens from outer space? What are we afraid of?"

"Who doesn't respect you? And why? I can't imagine."

He knew he had found the other side of her personality; it was the side that served as a ground for action and light-heartedness. Some people sink into that ground, others use it as a foundation to build on. He knew Jenny would never sink.

"Look ... what is this? How come I'm under the glass all of a sudden? I'm trying to tell you, you're a winner. There's big bucks in this place just waiting for you."

"That's horse-pucky." He was beginning to feel intimate with her. " Sounds like you're superstitious."

"Horse-pucky? Ha, ha, ha. I like that. Why didn't you say horse shit? You see? That's why I like you. You're funny and nice. Guys like you are too dumb to be losers."

"Wait a minute. Wait a minute. You got everything backwards." He blinked his eyes as if to put his brain in gear. "Uh ... you like me?"

"Well ... uh ... yeah ... sorta."

"And you say I'm funny. Talking to you is like talking to ... well, it's like talking to someone I've known for a long time.

58

You've got a way about you. I guess you really are open to strangers."

"There's that word again."

"Look, you're a good kid and ... yes, I do like your boobs, but ..."

"Ha, ha, ha. You see, King John? See how easy it is to open up with ... aliens?"

"King James, not King John. My friends use to call me the King James version; but you can call me Jim."

"OK, Jim; but now it's time to go make us some money." He was ready to yield, but knew better. It was strictly for suckers. There was nothing he'd like more than to walk out of this place with a bundle of money, but it never worked that way. No. He would not give in.

At first, her sparkling eyes beckoned; then she breathed heavily, and her whole body beckoned. He felt something inside caving in as he looked at her breasts and her smooth, delicate skin and said: "How could somebody from Colorado be so ..."

"Sexy?"

"Well, I picture Coloradans wearing tons of clothes to keep warm, not ... uh ... I mean, well ..."

"Boobs hanging out?"

"You really tell it like it is."

"Is that so bad?"

He had to think about that one, so he sipped on his coffee before he replied, "I think it's great."

"Unless you live in my home town. Say the wrong thing and somebody might be offended; look too sexy, and you're a slut."

"Is that what they called you," he blurted. Should have kept his mouth shut. "I mean, you're so free-spirited ... bouncy."

She wondered if he was just trying to be nice like all those two-faced phonies back home. She couldn't take another goody-goody; she had been deceived too many times. It was all sugar coating for passive-aggressives. Honesty, that's all she wanted; not New York ... rude, uncivilized ... just honest.

"Let's go get that jackpot. You're my luck."

He didn't budge. "Luck is for suckers."

"Is that what you think of me? I'm so dumb, I'm just another sucker?"

"Well, no. In your case it's superstition."

"OK, then tell me something Mr.Version: what do you believe in?"

She stared into his eyes waiting for an answer, and he knew he was about to get pinned down.

"Well? What do you believe in? God? Magic? What makes the universe tick?"

"Electrons," he answered quickly much to her surprise.

"And what makes electrons ... don't you see? Logic is not enough. This is not a common sense world. If we always had this stupid common sense attitude, we'd still be living in caves. There's something else out there; it's different from anything we know... and it's coming together. My dad could tell you. He was in tune with ..."

"In tune?" he said with a smirk.

"Forget it!"

"No, wait."

She stood up with a jolt and walked quickly toward the slot machines as he followed reluctantly. He was about to give up on her until she talked about the universe, and used that word: tuned.

"I didn't mean to insult your dad. Tell me what he ... "

"Some other time. Right now, you're my luck. It doesn't matter what you believe."

"That's crazy. I made you lose your jackpot. You call that luck?"

"That's my dues! You have to pay the gods before they pay you; but when they pay back ..."

Jim held his hands up. "You're nuts!"

They weaved through the crowd toward the machine with the progressive jackpot. It was open; and the numbers had gone up.

"Look! It's up to forty-four thousand, four hundred and forty-four. That's lucky! I told you. Put a dollar in ... quick."

"Me? I thought you ..."

"No. You have to do it. Don't you see that? What have I been trying to tell you?"

"I don't have the foggiest idea. What have you been trying to tell me?"

"You're the warrior. You have to go get it. You're the one ..."

"Get what?"

"Just play the machine! Do it! Hurry while the numbers are still lucky."

He knew it was useless to argue; you can't reason with superstition. Best to play it out ... let her see for herself.

She raised the cup of silver dollars in both hands as if it were a sacred chalice. Jim reached in and pulled a handful of coins out as he looked into her eyes. She was so sincere, serious, childlike; he hated to disappoint her. He dropped three coins into the slot as she watched with great intensity. Her heart beat faster, her lips parted, and her eyes flashed with the reflections of the casino.

He held another coin next to the slot ready to drop it in as soon as he lost. He was anxious to get it over with.

"See? Nothing." He pulled the handle again.

"Don't be in such a hurry."

He held another coin near the slot, and reached into the cup with his left hand in a show of pessimism. "Don't get so hyped. It's not gonna hit."

"Hey!" she screamed. "That's one!"

Jim looked at a lady and smiled. She smiled back and winked as if to ridicule Jenny's naiveté. He glanced at the coin in his hand, then pushed it half way into the slot to show the lady he was ready to pull again. He wasn't naive. Four genies? Never happen.

"Hah! That's two!"

Jim became uncomfortable as others watched. He liked her enthusiasm; but she didn't need to attract a crowd.

"We got three! One more time!"

Jim looked away, and the lady winked again. Lemons, cherries, genies ... it was just a blur as Jim turned his gaze skeptically, but irresistibly back to the machine. More people stretched to see the action; but they looked with pity as if they knew it wouldn't happen. Young people get so excited only to be disappointed.

"Don't get your hopes up, girl," a tall man said in a deep voice.

Jim's heart pounded. Would it just miss again?

Click.

Riinnngggg!

"Yahooooo!" Jenny screamed and leaped into the air. She grabbed Jim forcing him to drop the coin into the slot.

The tall man was stunned. "Forty-four thousand, four-hundred and forty-four dollars!"

Jim stood with his mouth open and said nothing.

"You won, John!" Jenny said in a squeaky voice. "You won! You won!"

"No, you ... it was your coin."

"You pulled it," she said with a big smile. "It was your luck; you gotta take it!"

"No. No ... I ..." He stared at the genies, still in disbelief, as the bell rang and people talked excitedly. He put his hand on the handle nervously as if he were ready to play again.

"Don't touch that!" a man called.

"Huh?"

Jenny leaped at his hand. She had just lost a jackpot, and she wouldn't let it happen again. In her excitement, she tripped and fell with both hands on his. The handle came down with a thud.

"Oh, my God!" a lady screamed. "Oh ... God! You did it again! You lost over forty thousand dollars."

With eyes bulging, Jenny said, "We played it off. We played it off. We play ..."

When people play slot machines, they don't stop for anything: fires, attempted robberies, heart-attack victims being carried off on stretchers, fights ... nothing stops the steady cadence of the slot machines. But this was unheard of. To play off a one thousand dollar jackpot was bad enough; but to play off forty grand just minutes later was a mortal sin. Everybody stopped pulling the handles. Security guards rushed to the scene. They wondered what horror would cause people to stand and stare, without a thought for their machines.

Jenny and Jim held their four hands together as they slid against the machine, and inched their way slowly to the floor. They sat staring at each other as the security guards stared down at them and the people looked on.

Jenny was the first to change the expression of horror on her face. First, the corner of her mouth turned up, then her cheeks puffed a little, finally, she laughed.

"You have a very square jaw. Ha, ha, ha."

He giggled and replied, "Yes, a very square ..." He laughed hysterically.

The security guards looked at each other, shook their heads and returned to their duties; but the people who watched were not so forgiving. They were here to get their jollies, and getting your jollies is serious business. You don't blow a forty thousand dollar jackpot. Why couldn't they hit it instead of these silly kids.

Jenny saw the anger in their faces. "John," she cautioned.

Jim stopped laughing. "Jim, not John."

"Let's get out of here." She grabbed his hand and helped him up.

People watched like mad dogs about to attack as she pulled him away. Their snarls and profanities caught Jim by surprise.

"Those people are really mad. What did we do to them?"

"Everything," Jenny said as she looked back over her shoulder. "I had a feeling we were about to be lynched."

Like a young woman in love, she held his hand and snuggled close as they walked.

"I don't understand, Jenny. First you're crazy over the big jackpot, then you act like it doesn't matter. I don't get you."

"Look, there's a nice restaurant on the other side away from the noise. Let me buy you some lunch."

"I'll buy ... I'm starved. I never finished my coffee."

People still watched as they stumbled down two stairs and around a corner. Jim glanced back self-consciously.

The restaurant seemed out of place; it lacked the mirrors, brass and noise of the gambling area. Earth colors, wood grain, and soft booths provided a comfortable atmosphere where Jenny could open up. As they waited to be seated, he glanced again at her voluptuous figure, while she stared into his eyes. Once again, she saw something powerful, magnificent. There seemed to be determination and honor in his face ... just like her dad. He felt her infatuation and tried to avoid it. He would have nothing more to do with this superstitious young lady ... as much as he would like to take advantage. If that's what she had in mind, he would make it clear that he would be on his way back to California as soon as he finished his lunch.

The menu offered a great selection; he was delighted to see his favorite food.

"Look. All the oysters you can eat. This is great. I never expected it from this place."

"Yuck! I'll take the ribs."

After they ordered, Jim leaned back and let out a big sigh. "We blew it."

"Nope."

"No! What do you mean, no?"

"We didn't blow anything."

"We didn't blow forty grand? You're telling me no? I could have uh... and you say no?"

She set her elbows on the table, slowly sunk her chin into her hands, and looked deep into his eyes. She did not need to search for anything in his face; she had already found it. Jim was puzzled by her behavior.

"You don't know anything, do you?" she said with a friendly smile.

"What do you mean?"

"I already explained. In fact, I proved it."

"Proved what?"

"Dues. I told you the first jackpot was just an offering to the gods. When you pay the gods, they pay back many times over; and that's exactly what they did. We lost one thousand, and got forty thousand."

"You're not only superstitious, you're demented. We lost the forty grand, remember?"

Jenny was delighted. The more he tried to reject her, the more she accepted him.

"Lady, you're full of contradictions. I tell you you're whacko, and you act as if you like it."

"You won't make me mad by calling me lady. For a while there, I thought you might be wishy-washy like those jerks in my home town.

If you call me a nut, at least it tells me you're honest and up-front. And as for the money, I already proved the gods pay handsomely if you offer a sacrifice. If one thousand got forty grand, just think what forty thousand will get us! That's our offering, and now they owe us."

"They?"

"It's gonna happen. I know it ... I can feel it ... I can see it in your face!" She was so excited, she lifted off her seat and dropped her palms flat down on the table.

People pretended not to hear; but Jim knew they were eavesdropping. He wanted to protect her from herself, but it was hopeless. Her innocence and expectation could only lead to disappointment. He would enjoy the oysters and leave.

"Don't clam up on me Jim. You're thinking you'll just humor me and make a fast exit. I hate deception, and I hate your silence. Call me anything you want; but spit it out."

He was surprised; she practically read his mind.

Robert Frauenhofer

"OK, you're right. So what do you want me to say?"

"Say what you feel," she said earnestly.

As the waitress placed a large helping of oysters in front of him, he found himself not caring anymore. If that's what she wanted ... fine.

He swallowed an oyster and said, "You got it, lady. You know how I feel? You're a crackpot!"

She smiled and chomped playfully on her spare ribs; her face and hands were covered with barbecue sauce.

"You like it!" His eyes squeezed in puzzlement; his voice was loud and uncontrolled. "I tell you you're nuts, and you like it." Then, in an abrupt change of tone, he said quietly, "You're face is a mess."

"It's very simple," she said in a calm, patient tone as if to explain to a child. "I don't like or dislike what you're saying, because I know you don't understand. What I do like is honesty. What I do like is to hear your feelings being expressed. What I do like is to know you care enough to open up. What I do like ..."

"Oh, shut up. What I do like, what I do like, what I do like ... you sound like a cuckoo clock. I don't care what you like; that's just the point. This is the real world, not Disneyland. See that little oyster in there? You know why I like those little guys so much? It's in my blood; I'm part Miwok Indian. That's where I got this square face. My ancestors lived on the coast and survived on clams and mussels. And now I knock on his shell and say, let me in my sweet, I want to eat you. But he says, go away ... what I do like is to be undisturbed ... what I do like is to sleep in peace. But I open him up, lift him to my mouth and go slurp." He swallowed with a show of delight. "Delicious. Now you are a part of me, and I don't care what you do like or don't like."

Jenny clapped her hands enthusiastically; barbecue sauce splashed from her palms. "Beautiful! I love it when you express yourself like that."

People looked and smiled, but Jim ignored them. He was wound up now, and he didn't care what anybody thought. He spoke as loud as he could so everybody could hear.

"You're not listening. What I'm trying to tell you is, I'll never see you again. I'm history. This game is over. A thousand dollars gone. Forty grand ... gone. The end. That's it. There is no more. That's all there is. The party's over. We blew it. We had our chance. How many ways do I have to say it?"

Jenny was too feisty to let it go unchallenged.

"Did you believe me when I dragged you back to that machine?" She talked with her hands, and waved a spare rib in the air. "Did I tell you my luck was bad until you came in? Did I tell you about the gods? Don't you know anything? Don't you know you're a warrior? How many ways do I have to say it?"

"Now you're showing off with sauce all over your face. And keep your voice down. You're in a restaurant."

"Me! If you can show off with your raunchy oysters, I can show off with my ribs."

He threw his hands in the air, looked up at the ceiling, and screamed. "Aaaahhhh!"

People stared and laughed at the spectacle made by these two young lovers.

"Well, I'm glad you got that out. Are you that frustrated? That's how you end it? Can't discuss it anymore?"

He sat quietly and stared at his oysters. When he looked up, her angry face told him she hated his silence.

He spoke quietly and deliberately as people turned back to their food and ignored them. "But you're being irrational. How can we discuss something so ridiculous?"

"Ridiculous? No. Anything you don't understand is ridiculous or radical, especially if it seems to go against your beloved common sense."

He decided to use another approach: be patient, listen, let her get it out. Sympathy and understanding ... that's what she needed.

"Well, I guess you're right. Some things are hard to understand."

She held a spare rib to her mouth; but the twinkle in her eyes revealed a hidden smile. She put it down and became very serious.

His sudden change of Heart was suspect, and she would hate it if he were condescending; but he deserved a reply.

"Well, maybe I should listen to what I'm saying. I've been talking a different language." She paused, then spoke decisively. "I'll just say one thing, and you get it or you don't. Go ahead and eat your oyster first."

He put it down to show respect. "No ... say what you want to say."

"Well, my daddy ... my dad ... back home, up there in the mountains ... he stood alone one day at the edge of a high cliff looking out at those awesome, snow covered Rockies, and ... never told anybody but me ... he listened to the sound of a gentle breeze as it descended into the valley below, and he heard ... his own voice. I mean, he literally ... I don't mean in the sense that you think ... I mean he really did hear the sound of his ... do you under ... can you understand?"

He stared at her in amazement, then smiled peacefully, stretched his body across the table and kissed her. "The sauce is delicious."

"So are you," she whispered. "Care for dessert?"

He wanted her now, but he would turn down the invitation. He had gained a new respect for her; but it was not respect that held him back. Sex must be personal; if not, you become de-personalized; you lose your identity and your will. He would not make the same mistake he had made before: sex first ... a person later. When he had sex for its own sake, something inside of him tried desperately to personalize it when it was over. He had to fall in love to save his spirit. If he walked away from it with no feeling for the person, he felt drained of his humanness. He was not some kind of machine with clogged pipes that had to be cleared. Sex? Oh yeah! But with a person, not a thing. Sure, it's just so much chemistry and pent up force; but you have to take nature's gift and extend it beyond the physical and emotional level, through the intellect, and on to the dizzying heights of the spirit where mere pleasure turns to ecstasy and delight. Only then is it complete; only there does a man come to know himself, his world, his meaning.

"I understand. Some other time."

"But, Jenny, there won't be another time. I'm going to California; you're going back to ... why are you looking at me like that?"

"I stopped here, but my destination is San Francisco. I want to volunteer ... the Pyramid."

"Look ... I... the pyramid? Uh, I don't know what you're thinking, Jenny, but ..."

"Yes you do."

"But ... you're not some cockerspaniel that followed me home from school."

"You're right. I'm half poodle."

He wanted to laugh, but he kept a serious face. "You're out of your mind."

"If it's your parents ..."

"No ... no parents." He spoke softly. "They live in Oregon."

With the most innocent face she could manage, she said, "You live alone?"

"Yes. Uh ... you mentioned the pyramid?"

"That's why I'm going to San Francisco."

He chuckled to himself as he thought about how he would explain all this to his friends. What kind of a day did I have? Well, I won a lot of money with this girl I never met, but we didn't win any money, and she wants to live with me, and her dad talks to the mountains, and she's here for the pyramid. Yeah, right.

"Look, I live in a little town north of San Francisco where the people don't like strangers."

"There's that word again."

"Well, you may not like it, but ..."

"Yeah, I know. You don't care what I do like, what I do like, what I do like."

She had learned the ways of the manipulators, and knew he would succumb to guilt. If it worked for Cockerspaniels, it could work for her. She put on a forlorn look and cocked her head like a puppy.

"But ... you can't be serious. You can't just go home with some total stranger. I could be ..."

"Yeah, I know ... a serial killer. You could be so clever that you can act dumb, and suck me into your trap. What better way to do it than to let me talk you into it instead of the other way around."

"Exactly. Jenny ... you shouldn't be so open to ... people you don't know."

"You're no serial killer, and you're no stranger. I've known you all my life."

"Fine. If you want to believe that ..." He stopped to think about it.

She leaned back, and pushed her plate away to indicate that she was finished eating, and ready to go with him. He knew she was serious, but it was out of the question.

"Look, what you don't understand is that Bolinas is a town where the people ..."

"Bolinas?"

"That's the town where I live. My parents bought a place there many years ago, and now I'm staying there. But the people there are very ... averse to strangers."

"Averse?"

"Let's put it this way: Bolinas would make a very nice tourist trap if that's what they wanted it to be; but instead, they remove the sign that tells how to get there so people can't find it. Everybody else wants tourist money, but they turn it away."

"You mean it's that hard to find?"

"There's only one road that leads out there."

"Out there? What is this, an island? I thought you said near San Francisco."

"It is. In fact, you can see the city lights from Bolinas at night. But it's a tough drive after you go over the gate. It's just after Stinson Beach on the other side of the bay."

"Over the gate?"

"The Golden Gate Bridge."

"Oh ... yes! I can't wait." She had never been to San Francisco, and could not contain herself.

Jim could not resist her child-like enthusiasm. "Well, I guess if you're going out there alone ... knowing you ... maybe you better have protection."

"Yeah!"

"But get all this other crap out of your mind ... warriors, winners, gods, magic. And you're not living with me, so whatever plans you have ... do you have a motel there? Any friends to stay with?"

"Don't worry, I'm fine."

Jim had a good heart, but he was not naive. He knew she would settle for an inch now and try for another when the time was right. "You came out here from Colorado ... no plans, no accommodations ... do you realize what could happen to you? What are you driving?"

"My dad gave me his 57 Chevy ... I like old cars."

He looked at her in disbelief. "Oh, no! You mean that white one I saw near the sign?"

"Of course. How many white 57 Chevy's are there?"

"Mine's red ... just like my face."

She laughed. He had just told her what she wanted to hear. It was another sign that they were meant for each other, and he knew she would interpret it that way.

"Now, Jenny. It doesn't mean a thing."

"I told you, didn't I? You won't listen. What does it take to make a believer out of you? I came in a white 57, and you came in just minutes behind me in a red one. What are the chances? Then we won that money and lost it. Why? There has to be a reason."

As she spoke, he remembered the riddle and the money. It was too obvious. Had to be more to it.

"What!" She said as she caught the look of puzzlement in his eyes.

"What what?"

"You remembered something. What is it?"

"Nothing."

She knew immediately he was lying; his face told it all. He was smart, talented, and good looking; but he was cursed with one weakness ... honesty.

"When I first saw you, I knew you weren't here to play poker. But that's OK, I won't press it. Let's go. I want to see your Chev."

He felt a little uncomfortable, knowing that she could read his face ... his mind. She seemed to pierce through his exterior, thin as it was, all the way down to his soul. But, somehow, it was OK for her ... no, not just OK, he liked it.

Like a warm glow emanating from a stove, her spirit warmed his, as it must have warmed everyone who experienced her presence. Even now, as he felt this way, she knew it; but they would pretend it wasn't so.

Could it be that fate had brought them together and the money was there for them to find? Out of the question; he couldn't keep it even if he found it. It didn't matter about the poll conducted by the chronicle which showed that eighty eight percent of the people would not turn it in if they found it. Recent tax hikes and rampant corruption at city hall had made people angry and bitter. Why should they turn it in so somebody else could steal it The madness continued in spite of the mayor. Treasure seekers stopped trying to hide the fact that they were looking for the money as people dug in the sand and looked behind rocks. The riddle said the top shelf; that could mean the top of a tree. Tree climbers defied the law and the mayor's warnings.

Jim put it out of his mind. He wasn't about to tell Jenny; she'd go bonkers.

He caressed her Chevy respectfully, but expressed his displeasure with the color.

"Why would anybody want to paint a beautiful machine like this white?"

"Why would anybody want to paint a beautiful machine like this red?" She stood with her hands on her hips as she looked disgustedly at his Chevy.

"Well, I can see we don't agree on anything. Mine has a nice deep throaty sound. I'll bet yours sounds like a wimp."

"So what are you trying to prove? Is this your phallic symbol? Your substitute? Where's the real thing?"

He turned and put his hand to his forehead in disbelief. "Hokay ... now you're really asking for it. Look, lady ..."

"Jim, will you listen to me? I don't care what color you paint your car. Let's just leave before we start a fight."

They agreed to meet at the Golden Gate Bridge if they got separated, but she would follow close behind. If they stopped only for coffee on the way, they would get there before dark.

She started her car quickly, and revved it for his benefit, staring at him head cocked, with a big grin. He listened to the deep throaty sound, as she stuck her tongue out, and motioned to him to lead the way.

She followed eagerly with complete faith in him, ready to put her past behind her, and start a new life. As she drove, she thought about the advice her dad had given her before he died: "Follow your fate. As each moment arrives, something inside tells you what it is. Trust it."

Jim watched the white Chevy in his rear view mirror, and couldn't help thinking how cute she looked behind the wheel. He liked her, but he was not ready for a relationship.

His mind seemed to pull in opposite directions, as if right-brain and left-brain were trying to strike a balance between logic and instinct, science and superstition. Thoughts of Rod Serling flashed through his mind. Here it is 2020, and they're still showing the old 'Twilight Zones'. He had seen every one at least twice; they had tremendous appeal for people like him. He was a wishful thinker, and he knew it.

His kind had always been easy game for con-artists, priests and witch doctors. They convince you that you have problems for which only they have the solutions. If they can make you believe in hell, purgatory or BO, you gotta buy salvation, indulgences or deodorant. Drop your coin in the box, and they put in a good word with the Lord.

His thoughts were interrupted by the news on the radio about the boy who fell from the bridge. He hoped Jenny had not heard it; best that she didn't know about the money.

It was a steep climb out of Reno, just the kind of place Jenny was used to. The Sierras look just like the Rockies in many places, pine trees, water gushing between rocks: she felt a twinge of nostalgia.

She passed Jim and signaled to pull over as she drove off the road into an opening between the trees.

"What the hell is she doing."

"Jim!" She shouted as she got out of the car.

"What are you stopping for? We're only a half hour out of Reno, and you're..."

"Listen!"

"What," he said, irritated. "I don't hear anything."

"Listen to the breeze moving through the trees. Isn't it romantic?"

"Romantic! You mean you stopped out here in the middle of BFE just to tell me ..." He looked into her bright eyes and knew what she had in mind. "Out here? You mean you ..." He looked back toward the road. "I can still see traffic from here."

She cropped the back of her hair with both hands thrusting her breast forward. She knew he could not resist.

"Jenny, I don't want sex without a relationship."

"You can have both."

"So ... you want to have sex in the back seat of my car? That's romantic for you?"

"No. It's this place. I love it," she said with arms outstretched.

"So ... you mean ..."

"Yes. Right there." She pointed at a soft spot on the ground covered with pine needles. Water trickled over mossy rocks next to plush green fern.

He laughed. "So this is your thing, doing it in the great outdoors. What if somebody pulls in here?"

She became defensive. "So what. Besides, you have your little thing, so I've got mine."

"My little ..."

"Yes. Boobs! It's pretty obvious you have a fetish for boobs. You checked every set that came along."

He was stunned. "Well, I ... all men ... I mean, we all look."

"Then look at these." She peeled her blouse as she stared into his eyes. Her bra moved slowly over her nipples as Jim stared with his mouth open.

"Gawd! No. Jenny ..."

She ignored him as she walked back to her car, took the keys out of the ignition, opened the trunk, and pulled out a blanket.

"Blanket."

"Jenny, you're fantastic, but ..."

"Blanket on ground. Clothes coming off. Naked lady. Remember, I'm a lady ... ah, there. Naked lady lying on chest, ass up."

"That's it!" He responded in kind. "Man taking off clothes. Cars going by."

She leaned on her elbow and watched him fumble nervously. "Man obviously risen to the occasion."

He spoke apologetically. "Well, there comes a point where you lose control. I'm only human; but I didn't want it to be like this."

She turned over and accepted him.

"NNgh, ooh. How did you want it to be?"

"Right now ... whoa ... I don't care."

"Losing control," she whispered, "that's what it's all about."

75

"Are you gonna stop talking and just ... oh ..."

"Why should I?" She never raised her voice over a whisper, even as she argued. "What's wrong with talking? You're telling me how it's supposed to be. What's wrong with ... woo ... just doing it? Why do we make a big deal out of everything. This is a romantic moment. Listen ... uh ... to the trees, smell the pine needles."

"Hear the cars, smell the smog."

"Oh, Jim."

"Oh, shut up."

"Is that all we ever do is argue? We're getting laid; I might even be getting pregnant at this very moment thanks to your unpreparedness, and ..."

"Ungh"

"Just keep doing it. Don't stop."

"You make me feel like I'm having ... mmm ...sex with a talking, wind-up ... doll."

"I'm not talking, I'm whispering ... like the trees."

"So I'm ... ooh ... making it with ... the trees."

"Yeah," she said in a long slow whisper.

"You're nuts."

Vanished

*J*enny was excited as she followed Jim into the parking lot near the Golden Gate Bridge. The red van was parked facing into the walkway where tourists gaped at the view. Don, Sarah and Candy sat motionless staring straight ahead. Jim pulled in to the left of the van; Jenny parked on their right.

Don watched the Red 57 Chevy, and listened as it revved once before it shut down; the white one revved twice. Normally, he would have been impressed; he would have gotten out and taken a closer look. But now it barely registered. Sarah watched as Jim and Jenny converged on the sidewalk and bounced along, their young faces beaming with delight.

She spoke softly to Don. "We will be like that again."

Jim waved his arms and said, "How's that for a view?"

"Look at that ship. It's humungous!"

He grabbed her hand and said, "Let's go, I'll show you the bridge; and then we'll go down to Baker Beach while it's still light."

"This is fantastic. What's the statue? Is that the guy who built it?" She pulled her hand back like a child resisting a parent.

"Yeah. We'll check it out later. Let's go."

"Oh, a gift shop."

"Forget it."

"Look at the flowers. This place is ... wow ... look at the bridge. This place is awesome."

Cars were still backed up; but everything else was back to normal. The crowd had dispersed, cop cars were gone, tourists came and went as if nothing had happened. As ships and tour-boats floated below, helicopters hung in the air above. In between, the bridge provided a fairy-tale walk into the sky that ended in a gray cloud. Cars moved abruptly from bright sunshine into dense fog.

"Look," Jenny said in a child like voice, "the tail lights disappear ... like they're going into another dimension."

"They are."

"Huh?"

"That's Marin County over there; that *is* another dimension. Come on. We'll walk half way. Traffic sure is moving slow ..."

"What is it? Jim ... you're looking weird again. What are you looking at?"

He stared at the bridge as if to focus his eyes.

"Come on." He pulled her until they were jogging together.

As they approached the infamous "jump" scene, he realized this was the very spot where it had happened. He stopped and looked for signs of blood.

"What are you looking for? You really are strange, you know that?"

"I told you, I could be some weirdo ... nut ... serial killer."

"Right. So what are you looking for?"

He ignored the question. "You have no doubts about me whatsoever, do you? Am I that tame? Is there no way I can scare you? What if I picked you up and threw you over the bridge?"

"I'm really scared," she said mockingly. "How 'bout if I take my clothes off first? At least I'd go out with a bang. I can see the headlines now. Man throws naked lady off bridge."

Jim shot back angrily. "OK, then how 'bout if I take you home, and show you my guns and knives?"

"Yes. Take me home. But why do you have to impress me with your manhood? What's wrong with tame? Some guys are tame until they're threatened ... then they turn into a tiger."

"Well, I guess that helps my ego a little."

He thought about it, but it didn't matter; he was more concerned about this place.

"So, why do you keep looking at the ground and ..."

"This is the spot."

"What spot?"

He suddenly remembered that she knew nothing about the death of Zack Pinches. Better not to say anything, especially about the money. She would find out sooner or later; but if he told her, she would rub it in about fate, magic, paying dues to the gods, and all that. In her mind, this would be the big one, the payoff. She would have him looking behind every tree. No way would they find the money, after everybody had searched for weeks.

"Uh ... this is the spot where that couple ... uh ... there was an accident here. You'll read about it in the papers."

She suddenly became very quiet, walked to the railing and looked down at the water as if mesmerized.

"Jenny."

When she did not respond, he walked over to her side. They gazed at the view together, but when he started to speak, she put her finger to her mouth and said, "shhh."

It's strange when you're on the bridge with all those people and all those cars. You'd expect the sounds to be different, like when you're in a crowded room. But if you listen closely, you probably won't hear anybody talking. The ocean seems to swallow the sound of the cars; even the thump, thump of their tires on the bridge seems to go with the wind to be taken out to sea. From here the sound of the ocean is soft ... the city is silent. You can see the skyline in the distance, you can see movement, cars, boats, joggers; you can feel the excitement of it's people. But it's too far away to be heard. If it could speak with one horrendous roar ... what would it say?

Sarah knew exactly what it would say ... I AM!

She had walked out onto the bridge alone; Don and Candy stayed in the van.

As she approached, she stared at this happy young couple who had pulled up in separate cars. They stood at exactly the same spot where everybody seemed to gravitate.

Suddenly, they felt the glare of her eyes on their backs. They turned in unison and looked into her face, a face so intense, they were compelled to move. Sarah walked to the railing, and stretched her arms out with her palms open, as if in prayer.

Jim was afraid she was a potential suicide; but Jenny recognized the strength in this woman's spirit.

They walked away, but Jim looked back, still worried, as Sarah put her arms down and felt the bridge with a gentle touch. The cold, hard steel was softened and smoothed over with paint. She turned and walked into the fog as Jim and Jenny watched her disappear.

"Well, I guess she's OK. What a beautiful woman ... she must be going through a sad time. We better get down to Baker Beach before it gets completely socked in."

As she walked by the red van parked between their cars, Jenny was impressed by its occupants. The man and the young girl stared out at the sky with the same intense eyes she had just seen in the woman on the bridge. The resemblance ... had to be the daughter.

When she started the white Chevy, she revved it until it snapped and popped. Jim held his hand to his nose to signal that he was not impressed.

She tail-gated him as they drove toward Baker Beach. He drove only a short distance down the road into the trees.

When they got out, she asked, "Why are we parking here? Where's the beach?"

"It's way down below; but we don't have too much daylight left, and they close the parking lot when it gets dark."

"How do we get down there?"

"Let's go." He grabbed her hand and pulled at a fast pace. "We'll walk the trail near the road. There's a way down after we get by these trees."

"Beach access!" Jenny read the sign enthusiastically. "Where? Oh! Down there? We're up high. What's this? Stairs?"

"Kinda." Jim stepped onto the logs first. "Careful."

Logs held together with cables were draped over the sands of the steep two-hundred foot drop down to the beach. Although it was a log-ladder, it was stretched out enough to make it almost as easy to climb as stairs.

The beach was still sunny, and the view of the bridge from there was made even more awesome by the fog as it pushed against the north coast.

"Wow! A bridge to the clouds!" Jenny said as she ran to the water's edge. "Are you sure Marin is really there, and it's not really another dimension?"

Jim gazed at the scene as if he had never been here before. As he watched the cars on the bridge, he said, "It's like it empties into nothingness ... like life and death. Cars come out of the void ... other cars go back into it."

"Is that where you live? Somewhere out there in that big gray mass of nothing?"

"Yup. Up the coast. If you had a powerful telescope ... we would have to be up higher, but ..."

"We would need more than altitude, we could use some daylight."

The sun seemed to set quickly as it always does when you don't want the day to end.

The entire beach was deserted, except for this fated couple who walked barefooted in the sand toward the bridge.

"I was hoping to get here earlier, " Jim said. "We better leave. It gets scary around here after the sun goes down."

"Wait! What was that?"

"What?"

"Way up there by that rock. Do the seals come up on the beach?"

"Seals! Now you're the one who's seeing things. Let's go. It's getting dark."

"No. I want to see it. It looked dark and slimy, it must have been alive, it ..."

She jumped onto the wet sand, and ran toward the rock as Jim stood with arms outstretched.

"What is she doing? Hey! Don't go out there by yourself!"

He could see her silhouette in the distance as she bent down behind the rock. The silhouette moved back and forth ... she was struggling.

"Jenny!"

He hurried to the wet sand where he could run faster, and approached the rock at full speed. "Jenny! Oh ... it's ..."

"He's just a boy ... must'a fell into the water. He's breathing," she said with her knees in the sand. "He seems to be all right."

Kevin coughed and opened his eyes. "My arm ... my arm. I got bit. Hurts ... bad."

"A stingray? Jelly fish? Turn around, Jenny ... don't look."
"What?"

"Just do it!" His square face seemed to bulge at the jaw.

She turned around, completely confused. Why would he want her not to look? Did he think she was so squeamish that she could not bear the sight of a simple wound? She turned back defiantly. "I'm not going to be treated like ..." She stared in disbelief. "Oh, my God! Are you nuts? You really are crazy!"

"I told you not to look!"

"You're ... you're ..."

"Yes! I'm pissing on his arm. Or, at least, I was trying to until you looked. Now you made me self-conscious, and I can't get it going again. Stop lookin' at it! I'll explain later."

She turned and sat in the sand. Maybe this was not such a good idea, after all. Her warrior was berserk.

"OK, you can turn around."

She looked cautiously as Jim rubbed urine on the wound.

"Urine is sterile; it's got something in it that relieves the pain of a bite like this."

Kevin agreed. "It doesn't sting so bad now."

Jenny sighed with relief. "How did you know that?"

"I told you about my ancestors. They knew a lot of things about survival."

"But ... what if they were wrong?"

"Couldn't do any harm. This kid's got a real stinger here. What happened? Where's your parents? Don't you know enough to stay away from these waves? Get sucked in by a sleeper, and it's adiose."

"The bridge ... cough ... hee, hee."

Jim held his hand out for support. "Can you sit up?"

He pulled himself up slowly and stared into space, glassy-eyed.

Jenny felt better about everything now: he was not seriously injured, and Jim was not crazy. "Where are your parents?"

Kevin's eyes expanded; he couldn't remember.

"What's your name?"

"I ... forgot."

"Give him a chance, Jenny. He needs to get everything in perspective."

"I'm not so sure. Do you remember where you live?"

"I ... can't remember."

"Try to remember your house, your parents."

"I can't ... but they must be ..."

"What? They must be what?"

"They must be ... rich."

"Oh, good." Jim said, as if there were nothing to be concerned about. "I'm sure they'll come back for you."

"Wait." Jenny was not satisfied. "Why do you say they must be rich? Aren't you sure?"

His eyes seemed to recede into his brain as he said, "Thirteen ... million. Thirteen ..."

"They're worth thirteen million?" Jim looked at Jenny and smiled. "I guess you could say they're ..." The smile seemed to slide off his face and his eyes dilated as he turned back to Kevin. "Thirteen mill ... uh." He looked back at Jenny with a give-away face which she could read like large print.

"Jim, what's going on?"

"Nothing."

"Wait a minute. Jim ... your face ... you're a lousy liar. What do you know about this?"

He ignored her and stared back into Kevin's eyes as he asked, "What about the money? What do you know about it?"

"I know. I know."

"Know what?" He was suddenly excited and filled with anticipation. "You know where it is?"

"Yes."

"Where?"

"I ... got it."

Jim calmed down. The boy was speaking from delirium; his injury was worse than a little bite.

Jenny looked around as if she thought there might be money all over the place. "The money? You asked him about ... the money? What money? You knew something all along. I told you! The stakes get higher every time. It's ..."

"You're wasting your time. He must have heard about it, and now he's ... delirious. He needs a doctor."

"Heard about it? Heard about it? Thirteen million dollars? Ah, ha, ha, ha. And why, may I ask, did you not tell me about this minor little detail?"

"Because I didn't want to hear about magic, and the gods, and all that crap."

"Precisely. You didn't want to hear the truth. I knew it. I knew it." She taunted him. "I told you so. Ah, ha, ha, ha, ha. Itolja, Itolja. This is what I do like, I do like, I do like. I'm a coo-coo clock. Coo-coo, coo-coo!" She was so excited she could not contain herself. "So tell me ... what's going on?"

"I'll explain everything; but, first, this guy needs a doctor." He turned to kevin and looked into his eyes. "Do you think you can walk?"

Kevin grabbed Jim's hand and stood up slowly. He twisted his body back and forth as a test. "I feel ... good." He walked in a circle, and knew he was in perfect shape, except for the sting on his arm.

Jim and Jenny decided not to ask any more questions until they got back to the car. Maybe a little walk would get the blood circulating again, and his memory would return. They walked quietly, except for an occasional remark by Jenny, who was very anxious to know the whole story. She wanted to grill Kevin, but she would cooperate with Jim ... at least until they got back to the car. In her excitement, she would get ahead, and have to slow down. Jim admired her hair ... something about that "cleaning-lady" hair-do looked great on her. Must have been because of the way her head bobbed up and down as she walked through the sand. She was lively, enthusiastic, childlike; but she would be disappointed if she tried to find the money.

Darkness seemed to move in faster than normal as Jim thought about the danger out here at night; every sleazy character in the area can see people on the beach from a distance, even in the dark; but from the beach you can't see into the darkness of the trees.

He looked around furtively; these lives were in his hands ... Jenny ... and this young kid ... just survived a near drowning ... wouldn't want him to get killed walking back through the trails. Where in the hell are his parents? Must be looking for him ... probably came down here on his own. The cars ... shouldn't have left them there so long.

"The stairs are over this way." Jenny said bubbling with excitement. "Come on."

"OK, but slow down. This guy needs to get his wind."

"I'm OK."

"Jenny! Don't go off by yourself! It's not safe out there!"

Her voice faded into the dark. "I'll wait for you at the top of the logs."

Jim reached for Kevin's arm. "Can you keep up?"

"I'm fine; but ... the arm."

"Sorry."

As they climbed the stairs, Jim realized that this young boy was in better shape than he was. It was a difficult climb ... much easier going down. The fog had moved in, and seemed to follow them up the stairs. Jim stopped half way up, and called, "Jenny!"

"There's no end to these steps," Kevin said as he looked back at Jim. "You need a rest?"

"No. Go 'head. Find her."

Kevin moved quickly as Jim struggled.

85

"She's not up here."

Jim hurried with all his strength, and made it to the top out of breath. A black pick-up truck sped through the fog on the road above. He figured she could have walked up to the road and bypassed the trail to the cars; it would be easier. He dismissed the idea; she never said she would.

"Damn! She's gotta be here." He looked around as Kevin stared into the fog. "She was only a couple of minutes ahead of us. Let's head for the cars. Follow me."

"I wonder if she went the wrong way ... down there." Kevin pointed to the trees above the beach to the south.

"She wouldn't go that way ... we parked up closer to the bridge."

He worried up more energy, and moved quickly up the trail. Kevin managed easily. In spite of the fall, he was filled with energy, as usual. They said nothing until they approached the opening in the trees.

"It's too dark ... I could swear we parked in this area. How could I be so stupid ... just because I didn't want to park in the parking lot."

Two '57 Chevy's in San Francisco ... just what the pro's are looking for. Should have known better. Jenny's so naive, and he didn't protect her. "I'm a jerk," he said aloud. If the cars had been stolen, she might have found them gone, and decided to rush back by way of the road instead of the trail; they would have missed her on the way. But now the cars were not important; the money was not important ... it was this beautiful young woman with the fantastic personality ... his future wife ... that's the only thing he cared about. He realized, in an instant, that he wanted to be with her always. To have her taken away like this ... to have this feeling that he may never see her again ... maybe that's what made him understand: once a person like this comes into your life, you can't live without them anymore.

"Please, God. I'll never take her for granted again."

Kevin looked sympathetically at Jim and said, "Where could she be?"

"You walk the trail back ... back the way we came." He was in a panic. "I'll take the road. Meet you there at the top of the stairs." They split up, Jim walking along the edge of the road calling Jenny, and Kevin walking the trail looking carefully in the shrubs for any sign of life. Jim was heart-broken when he saw Kevin waiting for him at the top of the stairs ... alone.

Kevin was the first to speak. "What if she went the other way by mistake?"

"She wouldn't." He felt a sense of horror. "Jenny ... you wouldn't!" He spoke to the fog. "Would you ... Jenny? She would. But why?" He wondered for only a few seconds why a person like that would do such a thing. The answer came in a flash. "She saw a spot where she thought the money might be, and went for it. Knowing her, she got it into her head ... like when you feel it in your bones. Jenny ... I'm gonna wring your neck."

Kevin listened with amusement; but he understood the dangers. "If she doesn't show up ... then what?"

"We'll have to search the trails through the trees ... down there, like you said."

"But it's too dark ... and the homeless people ... they sleep in there ... crazies."

"How did you know that?"

"I remember."

"Do you remember your name?"

Kevin stared into the fog as he tried hard to recall. "Thirteen ... mill ..."

"Do you really know where it is?"

"Yes."

"Where?"

"I don't know where it is, but ..."

"You just said you do ... now you don't. Which is it?"

"I ... know where it is ... in my mind. I can find it. But I don't know where it is ... I mean ... uh ..."

Amnesia ... must have had something to do with this delusion. He dismissed it, and focused on Jenny. "Maybe she fell someplace, and lost consciousness."

Kevin looked toward the trees. "We have to go down there," he said fearfully.

They walked slowly into the darkness, and whispered.

"I got a stick," Jim said. "Find another one. If anybody comes at us, swing for the face. I'll hit the knees. That'll stop 'em."

"This fog helps. Nobody can see us."

"Yeah, and we can't see them."

Jim felt like a child leading a child, but he was more concerned about Jenny than he was for his own safety. Nothing seemed real anymore. Maybe she was right, maybe fate had something in store for them and they had to pay their dues.

Big Mac

*T*he red van crossed the bridge, and parked at Vista Point on the Marin side.

Sarah refused to leave; they would sleep the night in the van. She walked out to the low stone wall, and gazed at the city lights across the bay. The blanket of fog had stopped on the bridge, but she could see the north tower clearly.

As Don sat in the van, he realized it was time for the Big Mac show. Mac Rogers did a night-time, talk show which was very popular in the Bay Area. It was not a time to be entertained; but Don turned the radio on hoping to hear some words of comfort. Mac was known for his forgiving and compassionate nature. The "Big" half of the nickname referred to his heart, not his size, even though he weighed in at a hefty 230 pounds. It all started when his callers repeatedly told him he had a good heart.

"Sooner or later, you're big heart will get you in trouble," a caller had said. "You care too much. You need to learn to be tough, rotten, mean. You're a loving and caring fool. Don't you know empathy is for losers?"

"You're certainly right ... no argument there. Now back to the issue ..."

"You jerk. What kind of philosophy is that? Are you one of those bleeding heart, altruistic do-gooders?"

"Not at all. But since you asked, I'll take this opportunity to sum up my philosophy for you: we all know what can happen on a battlefield. A soldier is shot as the platoon retreats to a bunker. It's dark, his voice cries out for help. The sergeant makes a tough decision ... they can't go back. The soldier will have to die rather than jeopardize the whole platoon. No argument from me ... it's the right thing to do. What would I do? Disobey orders. I'd go back."

"What if the platoon gets wiped out because of your stupidity?"

Without hesitation, Mac said, "If I die, it's my choice. If they follow, it's there's. If we all get killed, we're dead.

The caller could not believe anyone could think like this in today's world of greed and egoism. "That's stupid. With that kind of philosophy, a whole war could be lost."

"Right."

"You're nuts!"

"Could be."

"So you're Big Mac, the guy with the big heart ... can't leave a buddy to die, no matter what."

He laughed. "Big Mac? Well, you can call me anything you want ... would you want me in your platoon?"

"Are you kiddin'?" The voice paused. "Who would want a nut like you ... well, maybe."

Mac chuckled. "Then you're just as crazy as I am."

"I never said I was sane. Wouldn't be any fun."

In a friendly voice, Mac said, "But you said I was stupid."

"Right. So that makes two of us. Maybe ... maybe we're the only ones left who ... let's get back to the issue. What were we talking about?"

The name caught on: Mac Rogers was now Big Mac.

Don watched Sarah with her arm around Candy as he listened to the opening monologue:

"Crime and over-population produced an intolerable situation. So we built more prisons, which produced thousands and thousands of unemployable, half-out-of-their minds ex-cons, which has made homelessness and crime even worse. Oh, yeah, we've had some good times ... at their expense. The result? A sub-culture that won't go away, and a suicide cult that won't go away, and threatening us..

"Now we scream for the cops to protect us from all those bad guys out there. Well, folks, the police will be more than happy to give us what we want ... as they increase their power and control. We will beg for more laws, more regulations, more protection ... and get it. But as we pull in the ramparts against the hoards, we will lose the freedom to live ... without ramparts.

"Think about it.

"All over these beautiful hills of San Francisco, Sausalito, Tiburon and Mill Valley, I see thousands of houses that can never be called home. They are fortresses with iron gates, guard dogs, video cameras and alarm systems. We're living in little armed camps, each isolated from the next by plush landscapes designed to camouflage the stark reality of bigotry and greed. We surround ourselves with a cast of nannies, gardeners, and maids, mostly illegal immigrants, and we pretend to be living in an idealized, fifties type, "Leave it to Beaver" world. To protect this isolated ivory-tower life style, we hire our own gang of armed thugs; but we put uniforms on them, and call them cops.

"As we turn our backs on the cities, we fill our minds with excuses; but the truth is, we have made the cities what they are. We moved out because we decided we could not live next door to a black family, or in a neighborhood of Asians. The shame of our cities is the shame of our people. Little by little, our sins created this disgrace; and now it is there for the world to see.

"Is there a way out of this mess, or will we deteriorate further into chaos?

"The only answer? The pyramid."

Don's big ears twitched as if to listen harder; but Sarah interrupted without saying anything. From her position near the wall, she simply stared through the windshield, and he knew she wanted to tell him something.

He left the door open on the van and walked over to her. The radio was still playing, but not loud enough for her to hear.

"He's here ... somewhere around the bay. I can feel it. I feel his presence."

She smiled, and her eyes were radiant. She was truly happy, convinced that her instinct was correct. She would not leave as long as this feeling was as strong as it was.

Don returned to the van, and reached for the knob to turn the radio off, but stopped as Mac announced: "I have just been handed a news ... oh, no ... not again!

"Ladies and gentlemen, another purge has taken place. Several homeless people ... John ... are you there?"

"Yes, Mac. This is John Stiver at the corner of Bay and Stockton. Six bodies ... six more dead. Drive by. Witnesses said it was fast ... over in seconds. Six transients ... probably never got the message ... have been killed in what is, obviously, another purge. I never would have believed ... here, in America."

"I know how you feel, John," Mac consoled, "but, please ... just the report."

"Yes ... the report. Six dead bodies lie before me on the sidewalks and gutters, six dirty ... obviously transients, who strayed too close to the zone ... gunned down. Blood running down the gutter. And now, if this is not sickening enough, across the street, a crowd is gathering, and they're ..."

"Yeahhh!"

"YESSS!"

"YO MAMA!"

"They're cheering the deaths of these poor men who never had a chance."

"Boo. Boooooh!"

"POOR MEN, MY ASS! SCUM! THAT'S WHAT THEY ARE!

WE DON'T NEED 'EM AROUND HERE! This is WAR!

The crowd clapped and cheered, deliberately making it difficult for John to continue his report.

"Back to you, Mac," John shouted into the mike. "I don't think I want to be called an American anymore."

"THEN GET THE HELL OUT OF HERE," a woman shouted. "WE DON'T NEED YOU EITHER."

"Thank you, John. We'll get further details as they come in. See what you can learn; we'll get back to you when things settle down.

"There you have it, ladies and gentlemen, our country ... in the toilet. Like South American countries where they blow away homeless kids when they interfere with business, we have taken to purges like this bought and paid for by businessmen who won't tolerate the homeless when they get too close to the hot spots for tourists. Bay and Stockton is close to the forbidden zone at Fisherman's Wharf. They may have felt safe there, because it's far enough away not to bother anybody ... or maybe the shooters needed some extra money. We know they get paid according to how many 'head' they take out.

"I warned about this for years ... it had to happen. Our country is now among the list of depraved nations where this type of thing has become acceptable. More and more prisons, more money for the military, and less for education ... what did we expect? We created a huge subculture, and now, our own creation has become so intolerable that we ... cheer ... can you believe Americans ... cheer ... the slaughter of Americans. Good riddance, they say. Is this what the human race has been reduced to? I refuse to believe it.

"There has to be a place for everyone in society. We can't just throw people out like so much garbage. We can't do this! What have we become!

"And the answer is so simple ... the pyramid."

Don agreed. Why don't they just do it? He turned it off, and walked out to be with Sarah and Candy; listening to the radio had helped focus his mind away from the tragedy.

To lose a child is the worst, heart-rending tragedy parents can ever experience. To have a child fall from the Golden Gate Bridge is to add horror to devastation. Don had been so shaken, his body was only now beginning to stop trembling. Sarah had always said he didn't exercise enough discipline, especially with a kid like Kevin. If only they had stayed home; if only he had not allowed him to walk out there by himself ... if only ...

"Are you OK, Don?"

"I don't know. I ... my son ... I want my son."

"Don ... Don, if you've ever trusted me, trust me now. I know the pain you feel; but I swear to you with all my heart ... with all that I am, I tell you ... he's alive."

He searched her eyes for the truth. If she was in a state of denial, it certainly seemed to be working; she was calm and controlled.

She spoke assertively. "Scientists don't know everything. They predicted the end of religion; but, I tell you, religion is not dead ... it has just begun. There is something going on inside of us that we do not understand. Some kind of cosmic force flows through us."

He was beginning to believe she was right. By some miracle, Kevin could have survived. A mother's instinct is very powerful; if she could feel his presence, then he was alive. Maybe there really was a mother of all secrets, and she understood it. Maybe he had teased her unfairly all this time. Sarah's secret. Did she really know something the rest of us didn't know?

At that very moment, a black Ford pick-up with three passengers crossed the bridge to the north within several yards from where they stood. She glanced at it, unaware of the role it would play in her son's fate.

She may have known that he was alive, but she could not have known how he was involved in an adventure which would include thirteen million dollars.

The Dream

"**D**amn it, Mac! Enough is enough. If you don't get off this pyramid kick, you're history!"

Daryl Smyth, a thirty-five year-old, rich man's son, heir, elitist snob, and all-around egotistical ass-hole, lectured Mac Rogers on the perils of his crusade.

"We got volunteers calling us every day; they come from everywhere. What do we do with these people?" He turned his head, and spoke softly and disgustedly. "They're becoming a nuisance."

"A nuisance? People are just a nuisance?"

"Can't you see where this is leading?"

Mac was angry, but calm. "It's leading to ..."

"Failure! We'll be the laughing stock of the nation."

"Is that it? We might lose face? That's all that matters? Can't you see what this means? Do you realize how this nation can prosper? I know you own the station, but ... can't you see..."

"Pie-in-the-sky Utopianism! You got people believing ..."

"No! No, it is not! Every man who dreams a dream has to listen to the same old ridicule in those exact same words: pie-in-the-sky Utopianism! They told Strauss he couldn't build the Golden Gate Bridge. This is no different. It's not pie-in-the-sky. I'll tell you what it is, it's ..."

"No! I'll tell YOU what it is. It's your job, that's what it is." He poked a finger into Mac's soft chest.

Mac reeled and walked toward the door forcing Daryl to put-up or shut-up.

"All right. Look. I'll reconsider; but I want you to think about it.

I think it's time for a meeting, don't you? We'll discuss it."

Mac knew what that meant. A "meeting" was a hand-picked group already committed to a mind set which they would not change, no matter what. When Daryl could not have his way, he used this little trick to gang up on the dissenter. He knew how to bring people in line even as he convinced them they had something to say about it.

Sure, Mac thought, we'll discuss it. You'll twist my arm until you convert me.

"Why should I discuss it? I know I'm right, and you know I'm wrong."

"My God, Mac, why are you such a blockhead? Do you know what you're doing? Those people out there ... they have their hopes up because of you."

"Oh, isn't that terrible! For once, people might see some hope for the future of this country; for once, we are talking about a way to restore the energy and vitality of this nation; and we can't tolerate it because people might have hope. Hope! God damn it, that's what it's all about!"

"Stop shouting."

"You fat-head! What do you think made this country great in the first place?"

"For the love of Jesus Christ, God Almighty, Son of Mary and Joseph ... I don't want to lose you, Mac; but, so help me ..."

"You don't want to lose me? Or you don't want to lose your ratings?"

"Back off!"

"You don't seem to realize, it's not about my job, or your ratings." Mac's voice softened and smoothed out into a plea. "It's our country ... our country. It's going down the tubes. There's nothing left but damage control. We're in a damage control mode. We can't plug up the holes fast enough." He paused as Daryl got caught up in his emotion. "The subculture is enormous. We can't build enough jails. I know you're elitist by nature, but ..."

"Now see here ..."

"Let me finish, then give me your best shot. Punch me in the nose if you want to." He spoke calmly and deliberately. "You may have been born with the proverbial spoon in your mouth," Daryl choked on his words, as if they had come from his own mouth, "but there's still a man in there with a sense of decency."

"Oh, that's good of you."

"Then you've got to see that hope made this country great in the first place, and hope is the only thing ... the *only* thing that can restore that greatness. Hope! Hope-hope-hope-hope-hope! Can't you see that? Do you care?"

Daryl was beginning to show concern; but, empathy, a learned trait, comes very slowly to the elite.

"Do you care about our country? Or do you care only about your little kingdom here?"

Daryl waved his finger. "Look, Mac ... I wouldn't take this from anybody else ..."

"Then let me tell you something: it doesn't matter."

"Huh? What doesn't matter?"

"It doesn't matter if you care or not, because the pyramid cities will have a place for everybody, even elitists!"

"What? Are you suggesting an elitist society?"

"Not at all. The pyramid cities will bring greater freedom than ever before in the history of this nation ... and greater prosperity ... like we never imagined; but ..."

"More freedom? More?" Daryl sneered and walked around the room as if to show how disgusted he was with Mac's suggestion.. "You're going to put people in these boxes, and you call that freedom?"

"See? That's what pisses me off!"

"Stay calm. I'm trying to listen."

But Mac was excited and raised his voice. "Nobody gets put in boxes. That's typical Orwellaphobia. In the first place, nobody lives there who doesn't want to; in the second, consider yourself lucky if you can get in ... the waiting list will blow you away; in the third place, this will not happen overnight; in the fourth place, these homes ..."

"Homes?"

"Homes! Real homes! They'll assimilate single family homes in the suburbs with front and back yards, porches and decks, quiet neighborhoods. It's virtual reality at it's best. We'll have security, no crime ... you'll leave your doors unlocked."

"It's virtual all right; but it doesn't have anything to do with reality."

Mac paused and spoke calmly but assertively. "It will work! And all because enemy number one will be gone."

"Who's enemy number one?"

"Well ... not gone ... but out of the city."

"What are you saying?"

"The car! The stinking, noisy, gas guzzling, crime enabling, monster that produced urban sprawl, and destroyed the cities."

Daryl had him now. Talk like that made Mac's position completely untenable. "See, Mac? Do you see what I mean about you? You're so damn radical. You're out of synch."

"Me, out of synch?" He raised both hands in the air. "I see a world around me heading for Armageddon, I see homelessness everywhere in the midst of plenty, I see purges. And you know the worst part? You know what's worse than all that? Worse even than the suffering and misery? The worst of it is ..." He dropped his hands. "People are so numbed by it, they don't care anymore. And you say I'm out of synch? What about gridlock, smog, environmental destruction, crime, people driving an hour and more to work? Is that what you call synched up?" He pondered for a few seconds. "Mmm. You're right ... I am out of synch. I certainly hope so. I wouldn't want to be in synch with what's happening in this country today."

"You can't get along with an attitude like that," Daryl scolded.

Mac walked to the other side of the room and stared at the wall. When he turned around, he sighed and said, "Right. Go along, and get along ... that's what it's all about ain't it?"

"But, listen to yourself, Mac. You practically denounced your own country."

"Yes! I denounce this great country. I denounce the United States of America! Not for what it has been, but for what it has become. So there. I said it. Somebody had to say it."

"And, by God, you'd better not say it on the air!" Daryl shouted.

The Secret of Zen Ducks

"What happened to free speech?"

"I don't give a God damn about free speech; you are not ... not ... going to denounce this great country on my radio station. I'll blackball you so bad, you'll never work in this town again. Nobody's indispensable. They love you out there, but there's other lovable guys who..."

"Will you listen to me long enough to understand what I'm saying?" Mac said with deep emotion. "I will not denounce this country on your station or anybody else's."

"That's more like it." Daryl felt triumphant. He had put Mac in his place.

"But I will continue the crusade. We've got it all backwards ... that's why it's not working. Cars do not belong in cities, people do."

"Oh, Mac, Mac, Mac. You are so weird. No. Naive. Maybe that's why they love you so much. Always the optimist ... the idealist ... the Utopian. You say I'm an elitist; but maybe you're the one who's up there in an ivory tower. And from there, you can't see that people won't give up their cars; it's a love affair ... a passion. It's been fanned by advertisers who put sex and power into it. Don't you see that? The car means a lot more to people than just transportation. It's power, status, sex ... I mean, some people would feel downright impotent without a car."

"I understand that. Do you think I'm a dunce? They can have their cars outside the city where they belong ... not for everyday consumption."

Daryl would not even consider the possibility. "The whole concept is stupid; and I do not run a station for your benefit, so you can run your cockamamie crusade from my studio with my equipment."

Mac was pissed. A fair argument, even when it turned into a shouting match, was fine with him; but when Daryl started saying *my* station, and *my* stuff, Mac was tempted to take a hike. He controlled his temper, and tried another approach: "You think it's stupid? The people who live there won't think so when they enjoy a quality life, free from crime, and with plenty of leisure time to do as they please. In fact, even you won't think it's stupid when you enjoy your status."

"Status?" Mac had rung the bell that resonated for Daryl. "Status?"

"Yes ... status. Elitists like you will live on top of the pyramid with the biggest homes, so you can enjoy your status ... the thing you care about more than anything. The guy on the very top will have a penthouse view all around. His address will be number one."

Daryl thought about the idea; it was beginning to look a little better now ... more reasonable. "But, how ..."

"Simple. It's free enterprise, ain't it? The guy who can afford it gets the top spot. The lower the number of your address, the more status you have."

"If you can afford it."

"Just like it is now ... no different. Only difference is ... it's a pyramid, not urban sprawl, gridlock, smog, crime, noise, waste, etcetera, etcetada, etcetada."

Daryl thought about it for only a few seconds and shot back, "I'll see your etcetada, and raise you a few ... like, for instance, you're a dreamer, not a practical man; how do you get started; where's the financing; where do you build it; it's just plain crazy, etcetada, etcetada, etcetada."

"Crazy? Crazy you say? You wanna hear crazy? Lunatic? Look around. Gangs! Gridlock! Whole sections of cities are war zones where you dare not enter! That's crazy! How long did it take you to get here this morning? How long did you sit in traffic? That's crazy!"

"But, what if I don't want to live in your pyramids? I like the suburbs."

"All the *more* reason to support this rebuilding of the cities. If you want your suburbs to remain peaceful, urban sprawl must stop. How many nice, quiet little towns have been swallowed up ... even devastated by urban sprawl? Instead of strip-building, the businessman, the chains, and all that ... they could have space in the pyramid where they would operate much more efficiently."

Light bulbs clicked in Daryl's head. "Is that what this is all about, efficiency? I mean, isn't that what the Nazis ..."

"Nazis? If you say the word efficiency, why do you have to think Nazis? What about free enterprise? What about the industrial revolution? Aren't they about efficiency? Why do you think the world changed from medieval drudgery to a world of bounty? Because free enterprise is much more ... EFFICIENT ... than the old ways. The pyramid will be much more efficient than cities with suburbs. It will be more productive and competitive in a world where the ability to compete will decide who lives well, and who has to scratch. Medieval villages were paradise compared to ..."

"Medievalism," Daryl interrupted. "Why are you so obsessed with all this nonsense?" He thumped his buns into a chair disgustedly.

They both paused as if to take time to go back to their corners before coming out to center ring again.

Mac threw the first punch. "Don't you know what's happening out there? Think about it. Mass suicides, purges, the subculture. Doesn't it tell you something?"

"Sure, I've thought about it. The world's gone nuts. That's what's happening. It's a loony bin."

"No. Something else is happening, something so big ... nobody ... nothing can stop it."

Daryl sneered. "Gimmie a break. What do they gain by suicide? They're winning the war for us."

"No. It's part of their plan. Cults have always been with us, but this time they're unstoppable. Their fierce loyalty makes them a tremendous threat."

"Look, Mac. You don't understand these things. Cults, loyalty, they willingly give their lives for the cause, and all that; but they're brainwashed."

"But this time it's different. This time there's something else going on, something beyond the cult, something so big the

101

cult is just here to serve it. All the cults of the past have just been dress rehearsals. This is the real thing."

"Oh, my God, Mac. You're up a tree."

"Ridicule if you want, but ..."

"Then what? What's happening?"

"It's all coming together ... that's what."

Little Lady

*T*he black pick-up descended into the hills of Sausalito until it found it's way to the short driveway of a house overlooking the bay. Even here with the narrow, winding streets where people lived in close proximity, every inch of space was filled with ivy, shrubs and trees as if to hide and isolate the "neighbors" who never met. Residents ascended from their hide-aways, checked the mail, glanced furtively up and down the street, and returned to the safety of the den.

As always, fear controlled the world. We had descended from animals who peeked out of their caves in fear of their natural predators. Now we had embellished the caves, and developed guided missiles which we called cars. We could push a button, and zip into the cave from within the safety of the missile, and the garage door would close behind us.

We called it progress.

Sean spoke angrily. "Damn door is too slow. I thought you had it fixed."

Herbert answered timidly, "I did."

"Don't get out until the door is down behind us." Sean was concerned that neighbors might see his passenger.

Jenny had been forced to sit very low in the middle with duct tape over her mouth. They had developed the art of kidnapping to the point where it could be done in seconds, without a sound. A little duct tape and an iron grip by Herbert left potential witnesses unsure of the event which took place before their very eyes.

Once inside the house, Sean ordered Herbert to remove the tape.

"What do you want with me!" Jenny demanded.

"Let me introduce you to my friend, Herbert, the one who tore your blouse."

Herbert laughed. He couldn't wait to use her like a toy. He took his shirt off to impress her with his physique. She couldn't help looking at him, and he loved it. He could have won a Mr. America contest if it weren't for his grotesque face.

"I ain't never seen a set like that in my whole life. Gawd!"

He grabbed her breast, and she slapped his face.

"That was a mistake, little lady." Sean spoke with a smooth, silky voice. She had the feeling that he was slightly effeminate; but his pale, gaunt face scared her more than the huge, ugly man who lusted after her. "Herbert is very angry now."

"Why are you doing this to me?"

"Oh, I didn't tell you ... they call my big friend here, Herbert the pervert. I'm sure he will live up to his reputation before the night is over."

Herbert grinned. "Yeah, and when I'm through, you can have what's left."

"Ha, ha, ha." Sean's high-pitched laugh was sickening. He glared at her with his pale blue eyes and said, "Just bear in mind as Herbert plays his little games with you ... he's a gentleman compared to me."

"No, wait. My car. I got a '57 Chevy. You probably saw it near the beach. I'll give it to you."

"I didn't see any cars. Besides, a '57 Chevy in that area? Shit. It's gone by now. The pros have been working over-time lately."

She thought about the boy she was so eager to question just moments ago.

"The money. You must need money."

"Money? You'd like to make a donation to my church?"

"Yes ... a big donation."

Sean looked at Herbert and winked. He knew she was just stalling, but, why not? He loved cat-and-mouse.

"Oh, isn't that nice. I knew you were a generous person the minute I laid eyes on you. How much is a ... big ... donation?"

"I got somethin' big, little lady. Ha, ha, ha. And I'm gonna stick it right between your legs."

"Now, now, Herbert. Be nice. The lady wants to make a donation. Who knows, maybe she's got a nice fat bank account. You got an ATM?"

"No. Better than that."

"Ooooooh. She's big time. You got a big daddy?" Sean said as he searched her eyes for a lie. He would not be taken in by an obvious stall; but something about her made him feel as if he were looking at a beam of light seeping through a crack into the darkness of his mind.

"Big daddy? No, but I can help you get some big money."

He was beginning to believe her; but it would be out of character for him to appear even the least bit gullible. Still, she had an honest face. Maybe she had access to some big bucks. He would test her more before he gave her the benefit of the doubt. "Shall we stop playing games? I think it's time for the party to begin."

"Thirteen million!" She blurted as Herbert reached for her blouse.

"Huh?"

"Thirteen million dollars!"

"Don't give me that," Sean said with a half smile. "Are you trying to say you know where it is?"

Herbert stopped looking at her body, and looked at Sean for the first time since they entered the house. "She can't know where it is. I been all over the place. So's everybody else."

"But we did pick her up there ... and ... why was she running ... alone in the dark? Gorgeous chic like this ..."

"She was carrying her shoes when we picked her up." Herbert's eyes bulged with insight. "That's it. It's buried in the sand."

"I doubt it." Sean flicked his cigarette lighter, and held the flame near her face. "Have you ever heard of Agni?"

"Yes. Yes, I have. You mean the fire god?"

"Well! I'm impressed. Perhaps you would offer your body in sacrifice."

"Please ... no."

"If you know anything, I'd advise you to start talking ... and I mean now." Sean picked up a can of lighter fluid from the bar, took the top off and aped the motions of dousing her with it. Herbert went along with the charade; he pretended to light a match and throw it at her.

"I don't know where it is; but I know somebody who does."

"Oh, I get it. We talk to this person, and you tip 'em off." Sean's thin eyebrows came down hard into his eyes in an angry frown.

"She's just desperate."

"No!" She replied recklessly. "He's just a boy."

Herbert rejected the idea immediately. His chest swelled, and he breathed heavily. "A boy! Come off it. Lemmie at 'er."

"Wait!" Sean walked around the living room with a hand on his chin as he thought about it. "A boy ... you're saying a boy knows where the money is. Mmmm."

"She's lyin'."

"That's just it ... I can smell a lie. Problem is ... if she was lying, she would have said a friend ... anything. But ... a boy ... you don't just pick that out of nowhere ... especially when you're scared shitless. She's too young to be that good a liar. OK, suppose I buy your story, for now. How does this boy fit into the riddle?"

"Riddle? Uh ... the riddle ... of course."

"What? Wait a minute. You don't even know about the riddle."

"Of course I do."

"Tell us," Herbert demanded. "What's the riddle?"

"OK, I admit it. I don't know what you're talking about. I'm from Colorado ... I met this guy in Reno ... lives in Bol ... Bol ..."

"Bolinas."

"That's it. We drove here, and ..."

"Hold it. Slow down." Sean sensed that this young lady was real; but now there was another player, a guy she met in Reno. Was she baiting him? "I'm warning you," he said as he

106

grabbed her blouse and pulled her to his face, "if you think you can lead me around with lies ..."

"No. It's true. Look ... I'll just tell you everything I know."

As she babbled about the beach, and the boy who almost drowned, she looked around for something to use as a weapon. The fireplace poker ... if she could get it, she would swing for the big guy first. Go for the knees. Her dad always said, a man can't do any harm without knees.

She talked in desperation revealing everything she knew. "... and then Jim pissed on his arm."

Sean was convinced she was telling the truth.

"Wait!" Herbert gestured with his arms out; his chest heaved.

"Yes! That's the boy!" Sean said. "The one you saw. He must have survived the fall."

"The fall?" Jenny was confused. How could they have known?

"She's telling the truth. The rumors were true. The kid spotted the money, tried to reach it, and fell. They said they saw something go down with him. He held onto it! It floated! That must be how he survived. He knows where it is. It's true! Put your shirt on. We're gonna get us thirteen million dollars worth of clean money!"

With tape on her mouth, Jenny was forced again to sit low in the truck as the garage door opened. Herbert put his hand on her head and pushed down as she squirmed.

Somehow, he was beginning to feel something for this little lady, something he had never thought he could feel for a sexy young woman: respect.

Once again, they passed Vista Point where the red van and it's three passengers seemed to kneel in prayer at the altar of the city beyond.

The black pickup stopped near the road above Baker Beach, it's engine and lights off.

"Just sit tight for a while. Give us some time to check things out."

"What's the plan?" Herbert asked anxiously.

"We tape her hands in front of her and go down. Nobody can see us in this stuff."

She did not resist as the big man taped her wrists together. "It's really dark down there. If they're here, it ain't gonna be easy to find 'em."

He pulled her from the seat, and walked quickly behind Sean. It occurred to him that they may not be able to find the truck when they returned. He looked back, but it had already disappeared into the fog.

"First thing to do is check where you're parked. You said you met this guy in Reno. What was he driving? Take the tape off her mouth. If she tries anything, tape her up real quick. I'm warning you, little lady, try anything and you'll pay a steep price. It won't be worth the pain, believe me.."

Herbert tore the tape off viciously. Jenny flexed her lips to get rid of the sting. "He's driving a red '57 Chevy."

"I thought you said you were the one with the '57."

"Yes. Mine's white. His is red. That's why I knew it was my fate. It's not just a coincidence. We were meant for each other. He's a winner."

"Shut up."

They walked through the parking area; but there were no cars.

"He's gone," Herbert whispered. "Musta' took the kid to a doctor."

"No. He wouldn't leave without me. I know it. Somebody stole the cars."

"I believe the little lady is correct," Sean said as he looked around in the dark. "They're here, somewhere, searching for her. This should be fun. The hunt begins."

There seemed to be no ocean, only fog; but the sound was clear, and the fog horns which told boats where they were.

"But how we gonna find 'em out there in the dark?" Herbert asked.

"They're going to be as quiet as possible. Put the tape back on."

Herbert had his hand on her mouth before she could even think about screaming. He slipped his hand off, and plastered the tape immediately. "Practice makes perfect."

"Let's walk toward the trees; but stay back away from the main trail."

"It's so foggy, they can't see us, anyway."

"That's exactly what they're thinking. This is great," Sean said as he rubbed his hands together. "Just like a battle between submarines. Be quiet and listen for every sound."

The fog moved quickly from the shore like an eerie apparition hurrying to a death scene. Phantoms separated in sheets of fog, and fingered their way through the trees.

"What about the nuts who sleep in the bushes?"

"Anybody tries anything, pop 'em. If you can't stop them, my little pea-shooter here will take care of it; and it doesn't make any noise." Sean touched his hand to his chest.

They walked quietly through the trees, but Jenny tried to make noises by stepping on twigs. Herbert jerked her body into his to stop her.

He whispered, "Do it again, and you get a pain in the crotch." He put his hand on her thigh, and moved it inward to demonstrate. She pulled away as Sean looked back.

"Keep her under control," he whispered. "I heard something. I'm going ahead. Stay here with her."

Herbert stopped Sean with a big hand on his shoulder, and whispered, "Listen."

They froze. "Nothing."

"But I heard ..."

"Me too. Stay here."

Jenny suddenly pulled hard and broke loose; but she only managed to run a few feet before Herbert tackled her.

"Stay there on top of her. I'm going ahead."

"Yeah ... my pleasure."

As she looked up at the ugly face staring into her eyes, Jenny felt something for this hideous, evil man. Somewhere in there was a child, a mother's little boy; and only Jenny would see it at a time like this. Even now as she lay subdued, she saw into the heart of the man as she always saw into the hearts of people. They said she was naive, and she understood why; but she alone knew it was not naiveté. It wasn't that she could not see the evil in their hearts; she saw beyond it. She saw a place where few people would ever see, a place where the mind grows out of the spirit. Here, in this place, the soul would choose its direction.

Choice.

Does the seed choose to grow toward the sun? The answer could not be spoken. It was an answer only the soul could know, and it could only be sung in the song of life.

For an instant, Herbert saw something magnetic in her eyes. He blinked hard as if in recognition; but quickly put it out of his mind.

Sean moved like a cat through the trees. He peeked out from behind each tree before moving on. The chase. There was nothing more exciting; it was in his genes.

Jim and kevin had been all the way to the bridge and back; they were ready to give up. They walked the path confident that they were alone; but they were still cautious. When Sean saw their figures emerge from the fog, he pulled his gun, leaped in front of them and pointed it at Jim's chest.

"Gotcha!"

They stopped immediately, and raised their hands without being asked.

"Who are you? What do you want? I don't have any money."

"Ah, yes, but you will. And you are Jim, I presume. The man with the '57 Chev'."

"You ... you stole it. Where is it?"

"Herb! Over here!" he said without turning around.

Herbert got off of Jenny reluctantly and called, "Sean!"

"This way!"

He followed the voice in the fog, and pulled Jenny along. When she saw Jim, she tried to scream through the tape.

"Jenny! What have you done to her?"

"Nothing ... yet. If you care about your girl friend, you better lead us to the money."

Jim glanced at Kevin.

"We know about the boy. Where is it, kid?"

"That's him all right ... the kid with the water pistol."

"Water pistol?" Kevin said, confused.

"I saw you take the fall," Herbert said as he looked Kevin over for injuries. "I don't know how you made it."

"Fall?"

"We also know your memory is gone. She told us," Sean said as he waved the gun toward Jenny, "and the money, you know where it is."

"Don't tell them," Jim demanded. "Tell 'em now, and they have no reason to keep us alive. Set her free first."

Sean felt his temper burn in his head; but he controlled himself. They called him a hot-head; but he could keep his cool when he really wanted to. The money was more important than anything: He had to have it to finance his church. He felt his scarred hand and spoke angrily.

"Take the tape off."

"All of it?"

"Sure, why not? Let the lovers kiss."

Herbert pulled the tape hard. Jenny's wrists were sore; her lips stuck together. She wiped her mouth, and ran into Jim's arms.

"OK, kid, it's up to you. Where is it?"

"I don't know."

"Look, kid ... the little lady can die ... she's expendable." He pointed the gun at Jenny's head. "Now, you wouldn't want that on your conscience, would you?"

"But ... I don't know," Kevin said as he rubbed his temple. "I know where it is, but I don't know ... where it is."

111

Robert Frauenhofer

"What in the hell are you talking about?" Sean's patience was about to run out.

"I can see it ... in my mind ... the money ... but ... I ... I..."

Herbert was angry. "He's stallin'. He thinks we won't kill her."

Sean was more excited than he let on; he had to have the money. He would do anything to get it; but he would try the cautious approach ... not too threatening ... for now.

"Wait. It's dark now, anyway. I got a better idea. We're going back home. I come back tomorrow with the kid. You hold these two. Yeah ... that's it. We stay in touch with my cellular. The kid leads me to the money, and you don't let them go until I've got it."

Jim didn't like it. "Why should you let us go? Once we know where you live, we could lead the cops ..."

"No. We take care of that part real easy. We blind-fold you right now. Then we drive you around until you can't figure out where we are. The little lady has no idea where we live because her head was so low, she couldn't see anything but the dash board; and we took a little tour before we went home. She doesn't know if we live in Tiburon or San Rafael, or what. Only thing she knows is we're somewhere north of the bridge. Could be Sing-Sing for all she knows. Ha, ha, ha."

Herbert took his shirt off and tore it up to make blind folds; then he tied their hands behind their backs, and marched them up to the truck. Kevin was forced to sit on Jim's lap while Jenny sat on Herbert's. He molested her over Jim's objections, enjoying the domination as much as the sexual arousal.

As they drove, Sean drifted off into a world of his own. He had a mission ... to save the world; and now, fate was leading him to the money he needed to fulfill his destiny. He blamed science and religion for the condition of the world; people were influenced by one or the other:

Science turned people toward social Darwinism: if you can't make it, too bad. It was the law of the jungle all over again, except we had free enterprise as our latest excuse.

Religion turned people toward bigotry: our God is the only true God; our religion the only way to heaven.

In Sean's mind, religion was responsible for all the wars of the past, science was responsible for the dog-eat-dog attitude of the world today. Both of these forces had led to chaos; therefore, both were wrong. The only answer was another force, a force to which the human race must learn to pay homage, a force represented by the god, Agni.

Thrice born, he was born in heaven as the sun, born again in the atmosphere in the shape of lightning, and again on earth as the sacrificial fire and hearth fire.

"Consume!" Sean said out loud; his intensity pushed his thoughts into his vocal chords.

"Huh?"

"All things must be consumed."

Jim and Jenny were confused; but Herbert had heard it all before, and knew exactly what he was talking about.

Sean knew they would not listen; but the boy had a young, open mind ... he could be a disciple. He would be receptive to the truth which Sean alone possessed.

"Destruction is necessary for renewed creation. Can't you see it? It's so obvious."

He loved to preach. He pictured himself as a great orator who would save the world with his eloquent speech as he led people back to Agni.

Jenny decided to go along with him. "That's true," she said. "There can be no life without death."

"Yes, little lady. You know about Agni, consumer of flesh given in sacrifice. Agni. Agni is the answer, and I will make them see it. The world must understand before it's too late. Armageddon is just around the corner, and nothing can stop it except sacrifice!"

"But, how?" Jenny played along in the darkness of her blindfold. "How can you get people to listen ... about Agni?"

She could see that he was intelligent in his own way; but he was demented. His insanity provided him with focus; and focus

113

delivered insight. She remembered her dad saying: focus is power; dissipation is impotence. Maybe that was why so many crazies became powerful leaders.

She wanted to play to his ego, get on his good side; but she knew he was too clever for that. She would have to resign herself to him ... feed the hunger in him.

"My sparks have already begun to raise the awareness of ..."

"*Your* sparks!" Jim said.

"Sparks?" Jenny could not believe what she had gotten into. "You mean, you ..."

"Yes, little lady, me," Sean boasted of his achievement. "I started it, and now I must have the money to establish my church."

The subculture was ripe and ready to be exploited by a leader, and Sean saw himself as that man. It's one thing for people to be poor and still have the power of the ballot box; but quite another to be poor and powerless. It's one thing for people to be poor, and have hope provided by a great religion; but quite another to be hopeless. Here were masses of people who needed a leader to give them hope and power.

Agni was their only chance. They would have revenge when the country was devastated by nuclear bombs built and ready at Sean's command to be detonated by Sparks who would give their lives in the explosion. They would start with New York City. With several Sparks positioned, materials would be delivered a little at a time until they were ready. If one got caught, he would commit suicide, but others would be ready. It was insane, but with enough money, he was sure he could do it. After the first bomb, he could dictate his demands, and the country would have to submit to his will. He would have great power. Power!

"Then they'll listen," he blurted. "They'll do what I say. Tear down the prisons and release all those poor bastards. Give them decent homes to live in."

Jenny said nothing. She realized he was worse than she had thought. He was a madman.

As they passed Vista Point on the north side of the bridge, Sean said, "That's weird. Seems like that same red van has been there for a long time."

Herbert looked over. "That's the van that ..." he looked at Kevin who sat blind-folded and attentive.

He struggled with his memory. "Red van?" He saw the van in his mind just for an instant, then a kite, then it was gone.

Sean put a finger to his lips to silence Herbert who said no more.

Suddenly, Candy's quacking voice screamed from the van. "There he is! He's alive! That's him! Ma! Maaaa!"

"Candy! What's wrong? I thought you were asleep."

"Kevin! I just saw him! KEVINNNN!"

Don put his hand on her shoulder. "Settle down. You just had a dream."

"NOO! NOOO!" Her eyes were dilated to twice their normal size.

"Candy." Sarah spoke softly to calm her down. "There's nobody out there."

"Truck. He was in a truck!"

"How could you see him in a truck?"

"His head. Just the top of his head ... his hair ... the way it sticks up."

"Oh, honey, it could have been anybody. Lot's of boys his age have the same..."

"But mom ... I know it was him."

"Don't cry," Sarah said as she hugged her. "Go back to sleep."

To the north, San Quentin, more active than ever, loomed over the bay as a place of death for the evil ones. Executions had been increased to an average of two per week. Americans were no longer appalled; in fact, they seemed to be happy about it. Something in human nature has always needed revenge; it was a source of relief; like cool water on a severe burn.

Revenge. Sweet revenge. It made up for all the hurt we knew since we were born. We got even with our parents, teachers, employers, politicians, neighbors, everybody who ever hurt us in any way.

Put that demon to death.

Yes!

If there were no demons, we would create them; then, in our victory over them, we would say ... I Am!

Utopians did not understand this. They thought we could be satisfied, like contented cows, if everybody could be wealthy, and if machines did all the work. They did not understand that there had to be winners and losers. We could never be satisfied with a world full of winners only.

Sir Francis Drake Boulevard ... why not? Good place to turn off ... drive through some traffic, and back to 101 before returning to Sausalito.

On his return, Sean took the Spencer Avenue exit, and turned into the winding streets of ivy, shrubs, gates, walls and all those things which told the world that the people hidden behind them were too important to live openly where they could be seen.

Sean pushed the button, and waited impatiently as the door labored its way to the top.

"Don't move until that door is all the way down."

But something about the way he said it, for their benefit, made Jim realize that their little journey was just a charade. Sure, they didn't know where this place was, but they could still identify Sean and Herbert ... they would be easy to finger. Sean was playing this little game just to get the money. Once he got the boy alone, he would control him, pretend to release us; but we had to be ... dead.

"Tie 'em all on the two beds in the master bedroom. Stay awake and keep watch while I catch some z's. Early start in the morning."

He thought about a time when he couldn't find a house he had been to before. He circled around until he recognized something, and then he easily located the home. That must be why Kevin said he knows, but he doesn't know. He has to be in the area first. Then, when he recognizes something, it will come to him. Sean would sleep on it.

Herbert tied and taped Jim first, then Kevin on the same bed to his right.

"They ain't about to twitch a muscle, little lady. Now you. You get your own bed."

Jenny spoke in a very calm voice, as if she were a teacher, and Herbert a little schoolboy. "Until you get the money, you'd better not try anything with me. Sean would be very angry if you blew it. You can wait one more day ... and then ... I'm yours." She gazed at his shirtless physique with admiration, and he was pleased.

"OK, little lady ... you're worth the wait. But I gotta tie you up now."

He tied her slowly and lovingly as she looked into his eyes like a trusting child being put to bed; but, even as he looked at her, he did not see her. She knew he was fantasizing. He touched her gently and smiled. Was this his desire, to put a child to bed, and touch ... caress? She felt like a doll. That's it, she sensed; in his mind he's playing with dolls. She knew that it was best to be passive; the slightest rejection could lead to a violent explosion.

Herbert saw visions of a doll; but the one he saw lost its head, and he smashed it to pieces. Before he left the room, he touched her face. Jim turned his head and watched from the bed just a few feet away; but Herbert did not seem to be aware of his presence.

Jenny felt sorry for him; he had a twisted mind. As much as she despised the crimes which his type committed, she could reach out to this individual, empathize, and ... yes ... even love him.

As he turned into the hallway, he looked back like a concerned parent doting over a child. He left the door open, and went to the kitchen for a chair.

117

Jim spoke first. "Jenny. Are you all right?"

"Yes. Why does everybody call me lady? Ungh. This is gonna be one uncomfortable night. I can't move around."

"I know you didn't mean any of that sweet talk with our big friend."

"Quiet. He's back."

Herbert set the chair in front of the bedroom door, and faced it toward the living room. He walked away just long enough to turn the TV on. When he came back, he looked in on them and said, "You're not going anywhere. I'll be right back as soon as I get my shirt on, and make a sandwich."

Jim struggled with his bonds, but it was useless.

"Look ... kid," he said. "Whatever your name is ... there's something you need to understand. These guys ... they know we can identify them. If you lead them to the money ... we ... we're dead. They can't afford to let us walk. For that kind of money ... they're not gonna take any chances."

"You're right," Jenny said. "He's right. We have to think of a way out of this ..."

"Jenny, I didn't want to frighten you like that; but you need to know ... I mean ... these guys are nuts. Did you hear that guy? Agni? He thinks he's real."

"He is real."

"What!" He reeled his head to the left. Her face was only six feet from his. "You can't be serious. Is that what you meant about the gods, and all that ..."

"No, no, no. Listen. Agni is real, but not like you think I think he's real. I mean ... the spirit of Agni is real ... not like a ... ghost type spirit. I mean ... oh, forget it. Listen, maybe if I convince that guy ... what did Herbert call him?" She answered her own question. "Sean. If I can convince Sean like I believe in Agni ... like ... I'm willing to be a sacrifice ..."

"What? What are you saying?"

"I don't know. I'm just thinking out loud ... trying to buy time."

"I can help," Kevin said assertively.

"What? How?" Jim spoke to the ceiling in frustration. "You have to take them to the money sooner or later, or ..."

"No." Jenny said. "Don't risk your life. Play along until you get a chance to split. He sounds like he wants to make you a member of his church. You're young. He knows he can control you." She did not realize how high-spirited and independent he was.

"He ain't gonna control me. Even my parents couldn't do that."

"You remember?" Jenny asked.

"Oh ... no ... I just remembered ... I used to get in trouble."

Jim turned to the right and looked at Kevin's confused face. "Try. Try to remember. Maybe your name. Can you remember your name?"

"I ... I can't remember."

"How can you know where the money is if you can't even remember your name?"

"I just remember ... the shelf. The guy called it the top shelf."

"That's the riddle! Where is it? Where's the top shelf?"

"I ... don't know where it is. I just know ... when I know."

"Oh, God. You're not going to start that again."

"Don't push him, Jim. It takes time. Maybe after some sleep. Shhh. He's coming back."

Herbert sat down with a huge sandwich on a plate, and quickly became engrossed in a movie on TV.

"Jenny," Jim whispered. "We're gonna make it. We'll get out of this."

"But you don't really know me, Jim. As far as you know, I'm just some flaky lady who believes in gods ... which is not really what I believe. I mean, I do believe in gods, but I don't believe in ... well ... gods. You see? Every time I try to say it, it comes out as a complete contradiction."

"Maybe there is no other way to say it." Jim paused for thought. "But it doesn't matter. I don't care about your religion. I ..."

Robert Frauenhofer

"But it's not religion ... not like organized religion. There I go again. It's not religion as we know it. It's really religion ... I mean ... for real."

"For real?" Jim said disdainfully. "You mean regular religions ain't for real? Look ... I don't care ..."

"Sean knows, in his own way, about reality."

"Will you listen to me? I love you!"

"I know, but keep it down."

Herbert turned his head just for a second. He knew they were whispering to each other; but they were no threat. No need to do the tape thing on their mouths; they didn't have long to live, anyway.

"I know you love me, Jim; you don't have to say it. I even know why you love me, and why I love you. Furthermore, I knew we would be married long before you did. What took you so long?"

"You ... what?"

She smiled and looked back at the ceiling.

He forgot his bonds, and tried to get up to reach her.

"Damn!" He settled down and thought for a minute before he spoke again. "I don't get it. A minute ago, you said I didn't know you, and now ... just like that ..."

"Change your mind already?"

"Course not. I do know you. I already told you, I feel like I've known you all my life."

"And I've always known you. Now you know why I believe in ... whatever."

"In gods? What's that got to do with anything?"

"You'll see ... in time. Get some sleep. We'll think of a way out of this by morning."

But he woud not sleep all night. He thought about her body, her mind, her spirit ... especially her spirit. Yes, he knew why he loved her. There was something going on inside of her ... a mystery which he could not grasp.

He smiled as he thought, 'she's a puzzle ... a crossword puzzle ... and I have to do her.' But he knew that the crossword puzzles he did usually went unfinished. Maybe that's what he wanted. Always leave something to the imagination ... the unknown ... the mysterious.

Kevin had his own ideas about the next day. He hated being tied up. Once he got free, he would never let it happen again.

He felt a cricket in his hand, saw a seagull on a rail, and felt a wasp walking across his face. Freedom. For an instant, he knew what it was, and he smiled. He felt peaceful and calm. How could he be happy at a time like this? Of course. It was obvious ... if you listened.

Robert Frauenhofer

Baalbek

*T*he sun was about to set on the west bank of the Nile as snakes lifted their heads and absorbed the last rays of the day.

Waters were calm, air did not move.

In the stillness there was life; in life, all things were still.

In speech, nothing was said; in silence, all things were understood.

It was the city of Baalbek three thousand years before the birth of Christ; yet, all things living knew Him; only after His death would He be forgotten.

The people knew what was happening as they looked to the sky in expectation. They sensed what could not be spoken; their faces reflected joy.

A form appeared, but it was not form, it was color ... color to please the eye. But it was not color only, for color is vibration, and vibration is sound ... sound to please the ear. Yet, even as they listened, the sound became a smell, and then a taste.

Without touching the form, they could feel it, and they knew that all five senses were just one ... one single sense ... a sense which can bend and catch all things. Through this sense, they grasped the language of the universe expressed through nature; it was a vocabulary spoken by the trees, streams and rocks:

In bearing leaves and fruit which burst into all sorts of forms and textures, the tree says: I am this;

In gushing forth springs which flow and bubble and swirl, the earth says: I am this;

In giving birth which brings forth men and women, God says ... I am this.

Robert Frauenhofer

The Meek Shall Inherit the Earth

*A*s people expected to live longer, they became less tolerant of crime, overpopulation or anything which threatened their security. They were angry, and wanted the death penalty for rape, incest and manslaughter. Crime was increasing again, in spite of the fact that so many prisons had been built, and record numbers of people were behind bars. Haves and have-nots were polarized more than ever.

Freedom itself had been re-evaluated by professors, and discussed on talk shows throughout the country. They agreed that freedom and individualism had led to crime and chaos. Perhaps it was not necessary for everyone to be free ... or at least not to the extent we had known. After all, freedom had led many people through a confusing path of choices, which resulted in their *loss* of freedom ... if not in prison, then through a life of struggle. What good is freedom for those who turn it against themselves like a knife to the heart? Besides, there must come a point where crime can no longer be tolerated, even if it means that some people give up some of their freedom. They give it up anyway, if they go to jail.

As people demanded more protection, it became easier to rationalize. It was as if the professors had decided to rationalize for the politicians, who would do the bidding of the wealthy. Freedom, which had been diminished by laws necessary to regulate masses of people, would have to be diminished further.

Concepts like this could plunge freedom into a whirlpool; and the whirlpool was a toilet which could suck the whole country down.

Mac Rogers believed there was another way; his way, the pyramid, would restore order and preserve freedom.

This was the choice we had to make: to survive or not to survive.

Philosophers have said: there is no purpose to life except survival. To survive is the ultimate goal ... the only goal.

But there was something missing from the equation. Sean understood what it was ... in his own way.

Mac Rogers sensed it as he said, "I will die as a man before I will live as the ants." He spoke angrily. "I love the ants; they are an amazing species. But I am a man, and it is my destiny to reach higher. I can never be satisfied until I have found it ... IT ... the face of God, or whatever it is. Listen to music with great intensity, and you will hear it. You may see it in the eyes of a child, or you may find it hidden in the darkest regions of your greatest passion. But whatever it is, it touches the heart with such great power, that you know there is more than survival ... we are more than ants.

"Passion! Do ants have passion? There is no life for humans without it. Whatever you love most, do it with passion ... give yourself to it ... drown yourself in it ... die for it if necessary. When you have experienced your passion to its greatest intensity, then tell me if survival is the only goal ... or if there is something else."

As he signed off, he said, "And once again, remember ...

> 'sometimes naked, sometimes mad,
> now as a scholar, now as a fool.
> Thus, they appear on earth:
> The free men.'"

As usual, Mac was into high ideals and spiritual enlightenment, completely out of step with the times. Somehow, he knew, as did Sarah, that the Golden Gate Bridge was more than just a bridge. It was more like a ... church. Sarah's secret was here.

It basked in the light of the sun; the towers glowed and pierced the sky.

During construction in 1935, an earthquake had caused the south tower to sway back and forth like a hammock. Workers on top of the tower scuttled down as fast as they could; but several men had no choice but to lay on their stomachs and hold on. They all threw up as they watched the San Francisco skyline bob up and down. The towers had become gigantic tuning forks. They were stabilized after the cables were attached.

The old man still admired those cables even after all these years. He was in good form as he entertained tourists with squirrels crawling up his leg for nuts. On sundays, he was never surprised to see tourists out in force this early. Eight o'clock was a good time to be on the bridge, especially when the sun glistened against the San Francisco skyline.

"Yup. I been here all my life. Saw that bridge bein' built. Walked across it before the first car ever hit the pavement. It was a pipe dream back then. They said it couldn't be done. He showed 'em ... short little runt."

"Who?"

"That guy." He pointed to the statue of Joseph Strauss. "He built it."

A young woman stared at the bridge and said, "It doesn't seem real ... the way it glows."

"Maybe it ain't. Maybe it's just his dream, and we're all livin' in it."

Tourists laughed.

Suddenly, the squirrels ran away as if they had been spooked.

OOOOOOUUUUUUUMMMMMMM.

"What was that?"

"Yes!" The old man looked at the south tower. "Speak to me!"

"What was that?"

"The south tower. It vibrates just like ... vocal chords."

A few tourists ran from the bridge while others continued to walk, unconcerned. A fleeing tourist stopped next to the old man, and looked back. "Did you feel that?"

"Didn't feel it, but I sure heard it."

"Must have been an earthquake. I felt the bridge go up and down. I'd swear it lifted me right off the ground."

"No need to panic," the old man assured. He pointed to the south tower with his cane. "This baby's been through shakes before ... it can take anything ... believe me. It ain't goin' nowhere."

"I hope you're right."

"Of course he's right. Bridges give a little. No need to panic. Look at those people out there ... still walking around as if nothing happened. They never felt a thing."

"Yeah, but it sure moved more than a little where I was standing. I can tell you ... it moved big time!"

The old guy stroked his beard and smiled. "Go back out there and talk to it. It loves the attention."

"But, what was that noise?"

"Just the bridge singin' to ya."

"Sure, sure. But ... really, what was it?"

"I told ya, really. Ask the guys who work on it all the time. They'll tell ya, it's alive."

He pointed to the south tower with a finger back-handed over his shoulder. "Takes ten years to paint that tower right there. Those guys hear it singin' all the time. It hums. What you just heard was the loudest I ever heard it. Musta got to vibratin' from the shaker we just had. I'm tellin' ya, it's alive."

"Be serious. How can it be alive if it's just steel?"

"How can *you* be alive?"

"Huh?"

Another tourist seemed more concerned about the sensation in the press. "Hey, old man ... what do you know about all this stuff that's happening around here? What's this about floaters?"

"Floaters? Well, it's possible."

"Come on, old man. That's just a buncha ..."

"Look here, young man, all things are possible."

"All things?"

"All things ... are possible."

"That's easy for you to say, but how do you explain it?"

"I don't. But there those who say ... look ... what if somehow the earth's magnetic field shifted, and created anti gravity in certain spots at certain times?"

"Now you're stretchin' it."

"No. Think about it. The earth wobbles a little and the magnetic lines get a little separated momentarily. Result? No gravity at different places around the globe. Wouldn't know about it if it happened over the ocean. The bridge could be in a critical spot."

"You really believe that?"

"I believe one thing for sure. It's a nice day, and I intend to enjoy it while I can."

Tourists laughed and went on their way. His words were one thing, but his persona was another. No matter what he said, people always loved him. He was like a comfortable home where the atmosphere was so cozy and welcoming, you didn't care what the furniture looked like or what kind of literature filled the attic.

As they left, he noticed a faint glow over the horizon. It disappeared quickly; but he knew exactly what it was: St. Elmo's Fire. Earthquakes produce an electro-magnetic field, which creates a strange light over the earth. He thought about an old Japanese haiku:

> The earth speaks softly
> to the mountain
> which trembles
> and lights the sky.

Earthquakes, strange lights ... why do we need to explain these things in scientific terms. Does the earth not speak, the mountain tremble, and the sky light up?

He was partial to the more elegant expressions of primitive people. Their minds were not fragmented; they saw the unity in all things.

Modern man listened to science and turned it into a religion; we bowed before the altar of the almighty explanation. But the old man realized that, while science explains, it does not explain away. He had long ago developed the ability to see things in their wholeness. The function of science, on the other hand, is to dissect, separate, and classify. In doing so, scientists learn to abhor contradictions; yet, all things contain contradiction. Even lovers are opposites, but their embrace produces a mystical union which participates in the magic of creation. Every real thinker understands the need to open the mind to contradiction; all invention and discovery comes out of this energy.

Energy.

There seemed to be more of it here than anywhere else on the planet. It was fitting that this should be the most photographed area on earth. The earth loved it.

"It's OK, guys, it's over." He spoke to the squirrels who came out of hiding. "Our bridge is just singin' to ya. Feels like an interesting day, and it just started ... think I'll stick around."

As the red van pulled into a parking spot, the old man knew immediately who it was. He had watched Don race out of here the day before in search of his boy.

Sarah had decided to come back to the city side of the bridge to spend the day. She got out of the van and walked over to the railing where she could look out. The old man walked directly toward her. At first, she looked down at the squirrels that followed at his heels; then she looked directly into his eyes. His knowing smile took her by surprise; but his words were an even greater surprise.

"Fly the kite."

"What?" She spun around as he walked off. "What did you say?" But the old man was on his way down the hill toward Fort Point.

"That's it! Don! That's it! DON!"

She ran back to the van and leaped inside as she screamed, "Go! Go! I'll explain on the way!"

"Go where?"

"Crissey Field! No. Right down there on the Marina. I'm gonna fly the kite near the street. Everybody will see it. Kevin. He'll see it. How did he know?"

"How did who know what?"

"That old man with the squirrels. He said, 'fly the kite'. How could he know?"

"This is bananas!"

"I don't care. I'm staying there all day. You stay with Candy. Come back here after you leave me off. If you walk out on the bridge, you'll see the kite in the distance ... you'll know I'm there."

"What good will that do?"

"He's alive! He's looking for us. He'll see his kite."

As Don drove, he knew she needed to convince herself that she was doing something, somehow, to get her son back. He didn't want to trivialize her wild idea, but he left the radio on as if to maintain a level-head.

Mac Rogers commented on a report just in about an earthquake. Witnesses had said that the bridge made a strange noise, and moved up and down.

"We were just there," Don said.

"We were driving over it just about the time it happened."

Candy saw images in her mind of the bridge breaking up. "You mean, if the bridge fell down, we woulda' fell in the water like Kevin?"

"Candy. Of course not, " Sarah scolded as if she should not think the unthinkable. "The bridge is not going to fall down; it was built to hold up to any earthquake."

Don stopped next to the long grassy area near the street. From here, Sarah had a clear view of her bridge.

She pulled the kite from the back, and hurried off against the wind. It would be a struggle to get it up where others yanked strings and caused kites to dive, climb, swirl and hover.

She shouted through the wind. "What's this big hook on the end of the string!"

"Kevin always hooked it onto things so he wouldn't lose it!"

131

He closed the door, but didn't want to leave. "Are you sure you're OK?"

"Yes! Go! In case he returns to the bridge!" She waved him on, and pointed to the bridge as he drove off reluctantly.

He thought intensely about this great bridge. Why were so many people drawn to it? Why had his son died there, on that very spot where ... his mind wandered. 'Where two or more are gathered in my name' ... Sarah ... she had said, 'who are you?' Names. Gathered in my name, Holy Ghost.'

"That's it! My God! That's it!"

"Dad. What?"

"Sarah's secret. Nothing. Go back to sleep."

"I wasn't sleeping! Dad. Pay attention."

"Sleeping. Yes. The sleeping giant. But it's not China after all."

"China! What are you talking about, daddy."

"Nothing ... nothing. They called China the sleeping giant, that's all."

"But ... so what?"

"So what?" Don smiled. "I know now, that's what."

"Know what, dad?"

"What's happening ... I mean, what's really happening. Your mom was right ... Sarah's secret. I understand now. Religion is not dead ... it has just begun!"

"Oh, dad."

He stared straight ahead for a minute, then said, wistfully, "Oh, dad, oh daddo dad."

The Word Was Made Flesh

*P*udong: A rice paddy near Shanghai in the 1980's, now a thriving metropolis of five million people.

As the U.S. declined, China had continued to improve until 2005 when the world economy entered a period of stagnation. It was more than a flat spot on the economic cycle; the system itself was inadequate.

Free enterprise had produced tremendous success in China, but the quality of life had been overwhelmed by sheer numbers.

China was learning about numbers better than any country in the world; millions of people could never be dealt with as individuals. Too many people were like too many drops of water clinging to the inside of a container. When the numbers were great enough, *they* were no longer drops in a bucket; instead, *it* was a bucket of water.

China understood now, more than ever, that quality was desirable over quantity.

Only an economist would be foolish enough to explain quality in terms of quantity; but we don't take them seriously. Everybody knows an economist is a guy who sits with one foot in a freezer, the other foot in a stove, and says, 'On average, the temperature is just right'. He would probably place the Mona Lisa on a grid, analyze all the mathematical relationships, make some kind of correlation to the reaction of brain waves in terms of frequency and modulation, and be perfectly statisfied with his "explanation" of quality.

Numbers are one thing, but what about the real world?

In the real world of Pudong, gridlock was worse than ever, crime was increasing, and control of the masses by China's leaders was diminished.

Pudong had become a clear example of the enormous population and technology of the 21st century superimposed over 20th century thinking.

Wake up, China.

133

Wake up.

No.

Maybe what we are looking at is an egg; it's cracked and bursting with life.

Be BORN, China.

Be born ... born to a new age. Open your eyes, look around you, and see the new world.

Surprise! Overpopulation is not your worst problem; it's your greatest blessing!

Ironically, quality depends on quantity; but, once born, quality will go its own way.

Quantity was the mother who would give birth to the power of the people. Everywhere, as you gazed over the heads of the crowds, or listened to the noise of the traffic, you heard the moans of quantity; and from her womb, quality spoke in a whisper as it said ... I am.

Someday, she would be born, and she would cry for all to hear ... I AM!

Now China had the opportunity to reach into her womb and pull us into a new world. China, who had been first, even superior, in many things, could be first in the age of the pyramids.

But birth could only take place by one means, a means which could be summed up in one word, a word upon which the world must be focused, the word which must be made flesh and dwell amongst us.

Mac Rogers knew the word, and worked hard to deliver it into the world of light.

Pyramid Genes

*E*fficiency!" Mac Rogers knew the operant word for the 21st century. "It makes us truly human ."

A caller spoke angrily. "I don't know why so many people are involved in your pyramid scheme, it's ridiculous."

"Sir, it's not a pyramid scheme," Mac replied stiffly. "You make it sound like some Ponzi game. I'm talking about real pyramids ... like the pyramids of Egypt, only bigger and better."

"I know that, but I think it's stupid, and I can't understand why so many people are excited about it. You social planners are all the same with your Utopian regimentalism."

"Sir, not only is it not regimentation, it is precisely the opposite; we are losing our freedom. The pyramids will expand it ... more freedom than ever. And as for social planning, do you object when the so-called social planners prevent factories from being built next to your house?"

"That's only common sense."

"Why is it common sense when you like it, and social planning when you disagree?"

"Call it what you want, but I don't like all this hullabaloo. You got people all hyped up about this crap. It's like some kinda' spiritual thing."

"Maybe it is spiritual."

Just what the caller wanted him to say. "See? There you are. You admit you're a kook."

"Sir, just because you've never had a spiritual experience ..."

"Fine. If you believe in some kind of spirituality, that's your business. But keep it to yourself. I talk to people everyday who really believe in this nonsense. They got their hopes up. Young people think we're going to create some kind of perfect world where all we do is push buttons, live in luxury ... like the old cartoons ... the Jetsons. Don't you realize, we can't afford to build cities."

Robert Frauenhofer

"Can't afford it? Sir, we can't afford not to. Everyday, we are becoming more like a third world nation. More people in jail, more people in the streets. Civil war? Not likely. The police have the power to prevent it. But terrorism, riots, murders ... it only gets worse from here. The solution? Simple. Too simple. So simple, we won't do it: the pyramid. I'll preach it to anybody who will listen; I'll shout it from the rooftops. No sir, you're wrong, it's not a Utopian dream. It's just a better way to live. It makes a hell of a lot more sense than the chaos in the streets of our cities today. Given the advanced state of technology, the pyramid is, without question, an idea whose time has come. Think of it! No smog, no gridlock, no long commute. Imagine the time we will save ... time. Wouldn't you like to have more time in your life? Time to do the things you want to do? Look at the amount of time you waste commuting every day. Wouldn't it be nice ... and the convenience ... not to mention efficiency."

He spoke excitedly, as he always did when he got wound up about the concept of the pyramid.

"We could be so much more efficient, we could work four days a week, and take three off. We would travel more ... be more relaxed ... get more done in an hour."

The caller interrupted angrily. "Bozo's like you would have us all living in ant hills for the sake of efficiency."

Mac was steamed, but tried to stay calm. "Sir, I suggest you open your eyes, and see what's happening all around you. Efficiency is for people, not people for efficiency. Don't you realize, we can't make it anymore without efficiency. Yes! Efficiency. That's the word, the operant word for the new age. But it's not dehumanizing. Without efficiency, we work more, and life is drudgery, like the middle ages. Without efficiency, the subculture will grow; without efficiency ..."

"You're crazy! You got it backwards. Efficiency puts people out of work. It takes away ..."

"Yes! That's it exactly! And shouldn't it? Why do you want to work?"

"Huh?"

"Who says we must live in the new age by the standards of the old? I've got news for you, sir: the work ethic is dead ... dead and buried. It's been dead for a long time."

"You're bonkers."

"Don't you get it? Can't you see the handwriting on the wall? We need to work less, not more. And less, and less, until technology and machines do it all."

"But if you work less, you make less money."

"Yes, sir. And so does everybody else, which keeps prices low as technology becomes more efficient, which keeps production high. We produce more and more for less and less, and low prices translates into a pay raise."

"Well, it sounds good; but this is the real world. It's not that easy."

"Which is why we need to build pyramids where entire cities will be self-sufficient. Every home will be the very best quality with all the latest technology built in. Wall TV, stereo, computers ... you'll do your banking, mail, shopping, everything at the push of a button. Your home will have a great view from your terrace which will assimilate the back yard of a conventional single family home. Your back yard will be the roof of the one beneath you. That's why the city will be built as a pyramid. Everybody living in a pyramid city will be living in luxury, because efficiency will make the cities more competitive, and, therefore, wealthy. Do you want to live in a wealthy city, or a poor town?"

The caller chuckled. "You make it sound like moving into a wealthy neighborhood."

"Yes, sir, that's exactly what it is. right now, we have everything from wealthy neighborhoods all the way down to the ghettoes. Instead of building more low income housing, which only encourages poverty, why not build wealthy cities, wealthy because they're efficient, competitive, and productive; cities that give people the incentive to cooperate. Don't you see? That's why we have to do it. If we don't, other nations, like China, will produce pyramid cities so efficient, and so competitive, that, by comparison, we will be a backward nation."

His voice lifted to a higher octave, as if he were singing an opera. He couldn't hold back his enthusiasm; this is what he lived for. Something inside of him seemed to be programmed for this; and thousands of his listeners had the same feeling. It was as if the concept of the pyramids was part of our genetic code.

A woman called in and said, "Don't listen to that last caller, he doesn't understand. Either you know or you don't. Don't ask me why or how, but I've known this all my life. Something inside of me has always known about the pyramids; and you're helping to make it clear. Keep it up."

"I will. Think of the tremendous advantages ... ya' see ... I ... oh, God, I get so excited when I talk about this ... I don't know where to begin. Some people think I'm talkin' socialism. My God!" he shouted. "It's no more socialism than your local mall. You have competing businesses under one roof. Just because they share the same roof and the same parking lot doesn't make it socialism. It's free enterprise at its best. You can shop and play at your leisure, and you don't care if it's snowing out or if it's zero degrees out.

"Why can't we bring our homes together in a pyramid? Urban sprawl not only destroys the environment, it's expensive. It's a tremendous waste of time, energy, and money ... money we could use to build a better, stronger economy, and a better standard of living ... not to mention a lower crime rate, lower insurance rates, no more slaughter on the highways ... except on long weekends when we're all out there having a good time."

"I agree. I ..."

"We're wasting our wealth! Why can't people see that? We're wasting our wealth EVERY SINGLE DAY! When we learn to use our resources more efficiently, we will all live in affluence. Yes. There! I said it! I used that word, that big bad word ... efficiency! What do you think the industrial revolution was all about? Efficiency! That's right, folks. Efficiency! We learned to produce more and more without working from sun-up to sun-down in a life of drudgery. Now, we can break away even more! But we're stuck! The industrial revolution is stuck in second gear. We shifted from low to second when we got into the high tech information age; but now, we need to shift into high gear. Problem is, we have ... Orwellophobia. Some guy wrote a novel. Big deal. The pyramids won't regiment people ... exactly the opposite. They will set us free."

The caller continued to show her support. "Exactly. You're right on target, Mac. Nobody's twisting anybody's arm. You don't have to live anywhere you don't want to. I, for one, would be delighted to have the opportunity to live in your pyramid city. I'd love to have the peace and quiet of a city without cars, the convenience of everything together so I don't have to get in my car and drive everytime I need to go to a grocery store, or a restaurant, or whatever. And the feeling of security ..."

"Yes! It would be almost a return to the old days when they had the cop on the beat. You get to know the guy. Police protection becomes personal again. Your neighbor's son becomes a cop, and knows everybody, and everybody knows him. We're afraid the pyramid would be impersonal? Just the opposite! Today's world is impersonal! We're all isolated from each other. And you don't know the cop who is in that police car that drives by."

"Right. I would feel much safer and at ease in a quiet, clean environment where I can chat with the cop walking by. In fact, I think people would be friendlier; they wouldn't be in each other's way. Sometimes even friendly people become monsters when they get behind the wheel. Somebody cuts you off, or gives you the finger ... well, it changes your disposition. It's infectious."

"Good point. Listen, I'm out of time; but thank you for the call, and ..."

"One more point."

"Quickly."

"If we lived together in pyramids, which would be a return to the old village concept on a grand scale, wouldn't it be like playing on a team? I mean, we would have a stake in the fortunes, or misfortunes, of the city. What I'm saying is ... it's a way of life which encourages competition in the true spirit of free-enterprise; but it's a new form of competition which would also encourage cooperation. I mean ..."

"Exactly. In an overpopulated world, competition by individuals is not enough. We must have competition as teams. Uh ... I'd like to get into this more, but I gotta run."

Mac had been convinced for years that this was the true task of the 21st century. Yet, even he did not realize how awesome it was, or what it could lead to. Sarah knew it was not the ultimate goal, or the realization of our potential; it was just a beginning.

The new age was turning in the womb.

See the Gulls Float

*V*ista point on the San Francisco side of the bridge was more alive than ever. The air itself seemed to glow with energy. Flowers were brighter, leaves were luminescent, trees sparkled as the sun turned on and off through slits in the clouds.

Like a spotlight on a stage performer, the magic of creation itself was focused on the Golden Gate Bridge, while the world watched from the darkness of the mind.

Creation!

Light!

Energy!

It was here ... here where so many people had gathered in My name, where more energy had flowed into one place than anywhere on earth.

As Don drove into the parking lot, Candy bounced in her seat.

"I want to see mom's kite from the bridge!"

"Candy," he said in a voice clearly not intended to dissuade her. "Are you sure you want to walk out on the bridge where ... Kevin ..."

"It's OK, dad. He's alive; I saw him." She bounced out of the van.

Don moved quickly, and grabbed her hand as they walked. He held on tight as a sinking feeling reminded him of the trauma of losing Kevin. His feet seemed to get heavier and heavier as they approached the "spot".

He had not mentioned the fact that suicides from the bridge usually resulted in instant death on impact with the water. But now, he knew there was a chance that Kevin might have survived; and he needed to return to this place with his new found insight.

Suddenly, the weight in his feet began to lift. He felt the sensation of a weight moving up through his body as if he were in an elevator. When it reached the top of his head, it

141

disappeared, and he felt light again; but now, he felt lighter than before. He felt like a kite, and he suddenly feared that the wind would blow him off the bridge. He held onto a cable with one hand, and Candy with the other.

"There it is! There's mom!"

"How can you see ... oh ... it's the kite."

"Mom! Hi, mom!"

"She can't hear you, or even see you from this distance. His grip tightened on the cable as he felt lighter and lighter.

"Dad! What's happening!"

"Oh, my God! Hang on to me! Don't let go!"

They lifted off the bridge as tourists looked on in amazement.

"Floaters!"

"Get your camera!"

"I got it!"

Camcorders whirled, but the action was over in seconds. Don and Candy had floated in the air about ten feet above the bridge, then quickly descended. He had held Candy tight with one hand and wrapped the other arm around a vertical cable.

"I got it! I got it on tape!"

"It's a hoax! He rigged a cable on a pulley."

Don pulled Candy, and walked quickly.

"Dad, slow down! What's happening?"

"It's OK, let's just go."

A tourist shouted after them. "You're a phony. You're not fooling anybody. It's just a cheap stage trick."

Don knew it was real; but he wasn't in the mood to argue. He had no desire to be the center of attention at a time like this; he just wanted Kevin back.

"Now I know how Kevin survived. You were right, Candy, he's alive."

"Dad ... if we floated in the air, Kevin ..."

"Yes. He didn't climb on the railing, he floated. And he didn't slip and fall."

142

"I felt like a sea gull, dad. What happened to us? And I felt a ..."

"Nobody knows. But your mom ... maybe she ..."

"But how could they say we were lying; they saw us."

"Doesn't matter. People don't believe what they don't understand. I never believed it myself."

As they returned to the van, he recalled the stories about floaters who swore they lifted off the ground like a kite. Witnesses were usually present for the occurrence; but it always happened so quickly that they were not quite sure of what they saw.

The first such occurrence turned out to be a local magician, not at all believable. Those who followed were considered to be copy-cats who were either looking for attention, or trying to convince people that what they wanted to believe was real.

Every conceivable explanation was offered, from electromagnetic forces concentrated in one area of the globe, which offset the effects of gravity, to previews of the coming rapture.

One of the floaters, a very devout Christian woman, said that she experienced a state of ecstasy as she floated above the bridge, even though it lasted for only ten seconds.

"God has chosen this place to forewarn of the second coming," she had told the reporter who interviewed her on the bridge. "The rapture will soon take place, and we will be lifted up to heaven."

As they sat in the van, Don tried to recall some words from the bible.

"It's hard to explain what happened to us, Candy, but some people believe it has to do with the rapture. Do you remember learning about that?"

"I think so."

"I think the bible said: we will not all sleep, but we shall all be changed."

"What does that mean?"

"Well, Christians think we will be lifted up to heaven. Did you feel like you were going to heaven when you lifted up and floated like a bird?"

"No."

"Because it was something else."

"What?"

"It has to do with light and energy, and ... we'll discuss it with mom. We need to stay here and wait in case Kev comes back."

"He will." She stared at the bridge. "I wish I could do it again. I was scared, but I liked it. Now I know how it feels to be a sea gull."

Don often admired the sea gulls, and wished he could hover in the wind as they did. Now he knew what it was like. But there was something else happening here, something more important. It was as if something were trying to work it's way into our world from another dimension.

But why here ... always on the bridge. Murder, suicides, floaters. Maybe Sarah was right: Maybe there's more than what meets the eye. W.Y.S.I.W.Y.G.? Commonsenseville? Doesn't work anymore. The world would not understand if he tried to describe the way he had felt as he hovered over the bridge. It could not be explained ... nor understood.

But the sea gulls knew ... and the crickets, and the bees.

Jenny's Secret

*T*he quake went unnoticed in Sausalito where tourists hurried about eagerly. They crammed the streets like early-birds competing for crumbs. Couldn't walk, drive or park without fighting the crowds; yet, they loved it. Why did tourists struggle so hard to get their little piece of the action?

Maybe they didn't know.

A tall, thin man walked happily through the crowd waving and smiling. His straight, steady walk told everybody he had a purpose; his hat identified him as a man of obedience. It was a felt, cone-shaped hat with wooden matches hanging close together from its brim. It could have been worn, fittingly, by a sorcerer or a dunce; but, instead, it identified the wearer as something else: a phenomenon of the 21st century.

Tourists, known for their obnoxious behavior, generally walk directly in front of people, ignoring them as they point toward some attraction. They like to show off and play their phony little game of 'I'm-a-tourist-and-I-don't-even-see-you'; but, in this case, they quickly moved out of the way. Those who didn't, got bumped.

"You jerk! You splashed me with ... he's carrying an open can of gasoline!"

"Aagghh! Get out of the way! The hat! He's a spark!"

"Stop him!"

"Eeeeeeh! Stay away!"

The crowd retreated in all directions as he sat down on a curb. He moved around until he got comfortable, as if he intended to stay awhile ... a long while.

"Isn't someone going to do something?" a young woman asked.

"What for? They can't be stopped."

Others gathered to see what the attraction was, until the circle of people became an audience. Most people thought he was just another street mime about to go into his act.

"What's goin' on?" a man asked as he pushed his head over a woman's shoulder.

"Spark! He's a spark!"

"Ohmagawd. And ya'll just stand around and watch?"

"You wanna stop him, mister?"

"No, but ah ain't watchin' neithah. Ahm gown."

"Me neither. He's not going to ruin my whole day. I'm on vacation."

There were mixed emotions in the crowd: some were angry, some repulsed, some dispassionate; but they all watched.

"Kathy's not going to believe this," a woman said as if nothing concerned her except her own peers.

The man crossed his legs, doused himself with gasoline, and smiled as he lit a match.

"There goes another one!"

A lady shielded her son's eyes. "Don't look. Just remember, that's what happens when you do drugs."

"I know, ma. Oh, look. There's the ice cream shop we're looking for. Let's get a cone."

Smoke filled the air as the charred skeleton dropped into the gutter.

"Ugh! It smells awful."

Police cars arrived at the scene, and the crowd returned to their play as if nothing had happened.

The calm, sunny morning was suddenly interrupted by gusty winds as fast moving clouds quickly produced a canopy over the bay. The winds became stronger; tourists scampered for shelter. Within minutes, crowded streets became lonesome parking lots where only a few stranded souls waited in their cars for a change in the weather.

It would be a day of fierce winds around the bay, not what Sean had hoped for.

For Jenny, it would be a fateful day. She woke up when she heard Sean and Herbert arguing in the kitchen.

"You awake?" Jim asked.

"Uh ... yeah. What are they talking about?"

146

"I don't know. Can't make out what they're saying."

They strained to listen, but could not understand more than a few words now and then.

Herbert talked through toast and coffee as Sean made eggs and sausages.

"I just don't see why we have to ...'

"Don't gulp your food. You know what we have to do. You gettin' soft?"

"No ... but, she's such a neat little lady."

"She charmed you. She's no different than the rest. How many sausages?" Sean spoke casually of death and food as if he couldn't get excited about either.

"Yeah. Those are good."

"The whole package?"

"That all ya got?" Herbert sniffed.

"I got some bacon for me. We don't have to burn 'em ... until after they're dead. Look at those sausages sizzle."

"People are not sausages, ya know."

"Ha, ha, ha. You're a comedian. But you know what we gotta do. You can't keep her like she's some kinda doll. You can't put her on the shelf when you leave."

He understood Herbert's fantasies. He was a grown man with a reasonable level of intelligence; yet, his fantasies were infantile. Maybe they were right about those engrams ... maybe we were all it's victims, controlled by and through the microcosm.

"But ... I can't ..."

Sean spoke angrily. "You can do anything you put your mind to. I don't want to hear anymore of this! You know where you would be without me?"

"I know, but ..."

Sean raised his voice. "But nothing! We got a mission. Nothing gets in our way ... nothing!"

Jenny whispered, "I heard that."

"Me too," Kevin said.

"Shhh." Jim turned his head. "See if you can hear more."

147

Sean glanced toward the bedroom, and spoke softly. "You must realize how important this is; there are so many of us out there."

"But, killing ..."

"A few people are not important compared to the cause. Don't you see? If they knew how important this is, they would give their lives for it. Besides, murder is easy now; nobody cares."

"I know," Herbert said as he looked toward the bedroom. "Life is cheap. But ...Jenny."

"Jenny included! Everybody included! It's the way it is now ... the way it has to be. They don't worry about every little murder nowadays ... unless it's a big shot. People think we're doing them a favor if we kill off some of the excess population.

"They knew this day would come." Sean muttered, as if it were not necessary to speak clearly to Herbert. "Too many people. Now it's haves and have-nots. Had to happen. Except it's not the way they expected. Ha, ha, ha."

He spoke louder as he said, "Now it's big haves and little haves; and the little ones are falling through the cracks ... into our hands. They screwed themselves. There's no loyalty. Loyalty! Don't you see? Everything is a Ponzi game. You think your investment is safe until the guy before you needs your money. The game is screw-you. Now they need to get rid of people to protect their own interests."

Sean was ecstatic. "And that's where we come in. The survivors will be those who know the meaning of loyalty; the rest will eat themselves up. That's the message of the sparks ... absolute loyalty! We will be like ants on the march. Nothing can stop us!"

In Sean's mind, he was the new Messiah who would save the world. His religion, based on myth, would require sacrifice. Followers would willingly sacrifice their lives in public as a demonstration of the principles upon which his church was founded. He would organize the vast subculture into a single force until, like ants, they worked in absolute harmony.

Once the organization was in place, every single person in the country who had fallen through the cracks would know that there was a place to go where they could join the great cause; but once in, they could never back out. They would be required to give themselves completely to the cause, to die for it if necessary.

"And that's why we need that money. Thirteen million can go a long way in our organization."

Herbert agreed reluctantly. "I know, but Jenny ..."

"Do you believe in the cause?"

"Yes, but ... it's kinda like another Mafia."

"Except that it's a Mafia raised to the level of religion. It's the mother of all Mafiosi. Maybe this is what Mafiosi are all about; every Mafia requires absolute allegiance. Speaking of allegiance, just remember where you'd be without me ... in the gutter, instead of this nice house with your own gym room ... and sausages. Those done enough?"

"Maybe she would ... I mean ... she knows about Agni."

"Fine. Then she won't mind dying when I tell her she's a sacrifice. Ha, ha, ha. She'll realize what a privilege it is to serve."

"But you said you won't burn her alive."

"Sacrifices have to be alive. What kind of ritual would it be if I burned a cadaver?"

"Huh?"

"A dead body. OK ... fine. You can take the sad look off your face. We won't burn anybody. But when I give the word, I want 'em both dead. I'll take care of the boy."

Herbert hardly chewed his sausages; but it didn't matter, his mind was not focused enough to enjoy the taste.

Jenny could smell the aroma of sausage and bacon as it permeated the house. She thought about the fat and calories, how bad it was for her health. Then she realized that this could be her last day on earth. She inhaled the smell as if to absorb the last pleasure she would ever know.

149

Sean entered the room cautiously. When he was sure they were still tied tight, he released Kevin, and took him to the kitchen for breakfast. He looked back at Jenny with the most evil look she had ever seen in her life. She suddenly realized that, in his mind, she epitomized all that he hated.

Jim struggled as he spoke. "I'll get these things loose ... unnnh ... we'll make it."

"Always the optimist ... cavalier ... above it all."

"What do you mean?" He rested and waited for an explanation. She sounded like she woke up on the wrong side of the bed. Bad joke ... better not say it.

"Say what's in your heart," she said with a touch of anger. "We're afraid. Fear. We both know we could be dead before this day is over. Do we just play the game ... flippant ... right to the end?"

"Don't give up. We can do it."

"I'm not giving up. I'm just saying ... look ... we can't get loose, and, if we did, we got this huge goon ... armed, even ..."

"Don't think like that."

"Why? Because it's negative thinking? What about reality ... the real world? What's with men, anyway. Why can't you talk like real people? Why do I have to pry it out of you?"

"Pry what out of me? You're not making sense." He tried to keep his voice down.

"See? You don't even know what's in your own mind. Women are so easy to talk to. We express our feelings, we share our fears, we're intimate. You don't even know how to be intimate because you don't know what's going on inside. You're all covered up with images of your phony identity ... what you're *supposed* to be ... macho ... or whatever it is. You wear it like armor. You're afraid if you take it off, you'll be vulnerable. We'll see your weaknesses. People will laugh. God forbid ... people might laugh. There goes the male ego."

"Is this one of your woman's moods? I'm trying to get us out of this, and I gotta put up with one of your moods? Is this how you wake up in the morning? You need some coffee. Herbert will make breakfast for you."

"It's not about breakfast, and it's not a mood."

"Then what do you want from me?"

"Jim, I'm just saying ... learn how to say what's in your heart."

"OK, if that's what it takes to get you off this trip, how's this. I'm afraid. Course I'm afraid. What do you expect?"

"It's not a trip, and that's not enough. You ..."

"Not enough! What the hell do you want me to say?"

"Keep your voice down."

Sean walked in and checked the ropes again. "Lover's quarrel? Don't let me interrupt. We're leaving now. When the kid gets me the money, you walk. Herbert will take you into the kitchen for breakfast one at a time."

As he left, Jenny pushed on relentlessly; when she focused her mind on something, she was a bulldog, and Jim had to shake her loose.

"I'm just saying," she continued, "if men could just learn to be intimate ... you don't need to be a brute ... just let me know what's in there ... where you're coming from."

"I know what's eating you."

Jenny waited, but Jim said nothing.

"Well? What's ... eating me?"

"Jenny, can't we talk about this some other time?"

"See? There you go again. Clam up! Clam up before you expose the little guy in there who's afraid to come out of hiding. Sure, we're afraid for our lives; but there's a different kind of fear ... fear of being found out, fear of letting the world see who we really are."

That did it. Time to take the gloves off. "I'll tell you what's eating you. It has nothing to do with that. It's the test ... that's all."

"Test?"

"Yeah. And I'll tell you how women are. You told me how men are; now I'll tell you how women are. Cats. That's how

151

you are. The female fights the male, and forces him to dominate. He doesn't get his little pleasure unless he can hold her down. If he can't take her, he's not fit. He has to be strong. That way, the genes passed on are good, strong genes, and the species survives. It's her instinct to provide for her little kitties. They call it the instinct for the preservation of the species."

"No kiddin'. Do you think I don't know anything?"

"But that's exactly what women do to men. They nag, push and test. They want to know what we're made of."

"Jim, I'm not a cat. Women just want men to ..."

"I know what women want, and I know what they say they want ... two different things. You want to push me until I get pissed and say shut up. Then you'll know my strength, and you'll get off my case."

"That's not true. I just want intimacy and love."

They both stopped to think about it. Herbert had not been able to hear their words from the kitchen; but the steady sound of their voices told him that they were still secured. He perked up in the silence, but relaxed again when their talk resumed.

"Warrior." Jim spoke righteously. "Isn't that what you said? If I play the intimacy game, you'll be disappointed ... think I'm a wimp. If I seem flippant, so what? What do you want me to do? Shake in my boots and weep and tell you how scared I am and how unfair life is and poor me because when I was a boy my mommy did this and my daddy did that and my teacher scolded me and I bumped my knee? Oh, gosh, life is so tough. Let's all sit around and go over and over the whole thing. Screw that shit! I'm gettin' us out of this, and I don't care who you are or who I am or why or ..."

"Jim! Will you listen? If ... if we don't make it ... I just want to know who you really are. I'm just saying ... I want to know you."

Her words clamped down on his mind like a steel trap, and caught him for a moment. Finally, he replied with empathy. "You're worried. I understand."

"Who are you, Jim, tell me."

"I'm ... Jim King ... a student ... an aspiring engineer."

"No. Take away the labels. No labels."

"What do you mean, no labels?

Jenny thought carefully. "Everybody says, I'm a teacher, a housewife, whatever. But ... what if you remove all the labels? Don't define yourself by your status, your job, or any of that surface stuff. Who are you, really? Without the labels, do you still exist?"

"Of course. I'm still me."

"But that doesn't tell me anything. Go down deep into yourself. Feel your own presence."

He was more cooperative now. "OK, I can do that. It's like meditation."

"When you're in that space, do you know who you are?"

"Yes." He paused, then contradicted himself. "No. But I know who I am not."

"Who are you not?"

"I am not ..." His eyes almost seemed to click as his thoughts slipped from one space to another. Finally, when he regained traction, he said, "I'm not a student ... or an aspiring engineer." He spoke with astonishment at his discovery.

Jenny smiled.

"I think I understand. It's not just a test. You want to open me up until you find the spirit inside me."

"Yes. The spirit in me greets the spirit in you."

"I like your little game." He realized that she was in the realm of religion; but it seemed more real than ever. "But, while we're peeling away the layers of surface stuff, tell me about you. I don't want to die without knowing more about you. What about Colorado? Why are you here ... alone? Where's your family?"

"I have a sister who ... won't speak to me."

"Why? Fa God's sake! A happy, vibrant person like you. Did you do drugs, booze ... what?"

"No. It was ... bad, real bad." She choked on bad. "I ... maybe this is not the time. We need to think about our escape."

153

"Our escape will come at the right time. Just be prepared, observant ... a split second ... hit him with something. But, tell me ... tell me now. Let it out."

She took a deep breath, and spoke with great effort. "It's ... horrible." Her voice cracked. "It's so hard to talk about. You may think differently of me if ..."

"All the more reason to tell me. Put our love to the test. Release it ... it's not that bad."

"That's what you think." Tears flooded her eyes. "Just thinking about it hurts so bad inside ..."

"Let it out ... every detail." Jim was pulled between sympathy and morbid curiosity.

"I ... I'll make it short." She thought for a minute, as if to compact her thoughts. "My sister's boy friend ... sexy ... lively ... practical joker. He was ... in our hot tub one day. I walked out onto the deck ... didn't know he was there. Well, out there where we live, there are no neighbors; we just take a quick shower, and walk out to the tub. I had nothing on ... neither did he. When I saw his head turn ... that's all I could see ... just his head above the water ... I let out a scream, and then realized it was him. But ... he did a dumb thing; instead of staying there, he jumped out. I ran into the bedroom, and ... being the type of person he was ... crazy ... crazy Alex ... why? Why did you have to be such a jerk, but such a nice jerk?"

"What happened?"

Her voice shook with emotion. "He reached down where his clothes were, and picked up a fake ... rubber knife ... typical for him to have it. Then he came in and held the knife up as if to threaten me. I told him to stop acting like a weirdo, and put some clothes on; but he came closer, giggled ... he was having great fun. That's how he was. I backed away, and fell down on the bed. That's where he should have stopped. He should ... but he came down on me ... I mean ... we were in ... position. But, he had no ..." She choked on her tears, and could not continue.

"It's OK, Jenny; say it. Take your time, but say it."

"He had no ... erection. Maybe ... the hot tub ... he was relaxed ... glass of wine was empty."

Jim replied with words of support. "He must have been in a good mood. Maybe he was buzzed up a little."

"Maybe. But, he kept laughing. He lifted the knife, and pretended to stab me. Just as his arm came down ..."

She lost her composure, and could not say the words.

"What happened?"

"A shot."

"Oh, Jenny, no. Oh, God, I wish I could hold you right now."

"My dad had heard the scream from downstairs, grabbed a gun, and ran up. With the high crime rate, you have to be armed if you live far away from police protection."

"Of course," Jim replied as if to soothe her.

She continued slowly. "When he ran into the bedroom ... in that split second ... he saw the knife coming down on me. Imagine his horror when he saw a naked man ... and the knife. His daughter was being murdered. He just pulled the trigger; he didn't think or aim."

"I can imagine your horror when ..."

"Oh, God. The side of his head ..." She stared at her thoughts on the ceiling. "Gone!" She cried, and Jim waited patiently until she spoke again.

"And you know what went through my mind in that horrible instant? I know it sounds crazy ..."

"Say it," Jim nudged.

"Halloween." She closed her eyes. "I dropped a pumpkin once. It split open on the concrete. The seeds had not been cleaned out yet. One side came off." She opened here eyes and said, "Am I crazy?"

"No, you're not crazy. It was the trauma."

"That's all I could see, clear as can be ... a pumpkin. Then I fainted."

There was a long silence as she regained her composure. She swallowed tears, and determined to control her emotions.

155

Jim maintained silence out of respect. Finally, when she spoke again, she was calm and detached.

"My dad never faced charges, obviously. But my sister blamed me. I was always the sexy one, always horsing around. But it wasn't me; Alex was a real joker. I don't know for sure what his intentions were that day. It was all so spontaneous. Well ... I stayed a year after that. My dad died ... it hurt him bad to see his daughters ... enemies."

"Where's your mom?" Jim hesitated, and spoke cautiously. "Divorce?"

"She died five years ago in an accident."

"So your dad died, and you decided to go west."

"He said ... go on living ... do it for me. After I grieved, I decided to take the money from the house, and go do my thing."

"What is your thing?"

"I will follow my fate. It will lead me ... it will tell me."

"Jenny, you must ... we must return to your sister ... be friends again."

"Maybe, someday. Right now, we need to ... right now, I hear the big guy."

As Herbert entered, he looked lovingly at Jenny, and ignored Jim. He untied her with the soft touch of a kitten.

"Good morning, little lady. I have your breakfast all made and on the table. I know you must be hungry and uncomfortable."

She got up and stretched as Jim caught her glance, and struggled with the ropes.

Herbert enjoyed his coffee in her company until she stopped eating, and looked directly into his eyes.

"You're going to kill us."

"No."

"You're lying."

"I don't ... no, I don't want to kill you."

"I know you don't." She put her hand on his. "But Sean will make you do it."

"He can't make me ... but, I ..."

"Yes. You have to. Is that what he told you?"

He looked down with a feeling of shame as she pulled her hand back.

"What is this church he wants to build?"

"It's just ... has to do with death."

"Well, I guess all churches deal with death. That's why we have churches."

"That's what Sean said. But they don't really deal with it. He said ... they avoid it."

"They do?" She pondered over his words for just a few seconds. "They do. Yes."

"They pretend we're all gonna live forever. Do you believe that?"

She nibbled on her toast and wondered why he had asked. Was he searching for answers? "I believe ... well, there's only one way to say it. It may sound strange, but ..."

"That's OK, Sean says funny things all the time."

He had opened the door; he wanted to hear what she would say. Maybe he was looking for an excuse to spare her. She had nothing to lose if she opened up to him.

"Well ... there never was a time when I was not."

"Huh?"

"And there will never be a time when I will not be."

"Uh ... that's ... um ..." Herbert was confused.

"And I can never die."

"You can never die?"

"Nope. And you know why?"

"Why?"

"Because I was never born."

He smiled; she must be joking.

Well, you asked me what I believe." She spoke indignantly.

When he realized she was serious, he wanted to ask her to explain; but she questioned him instead.

"How does Sean's church deal with death?"

"He says ... just face right up to it. If we make human sacrifices ... well, I guess it helps us understand death, and deal with it."

"In a way, that makes sense." She spoke as if to herself. "People who appreciate death also appreciate life ... every precious moment of it. In fact, when you think about it, we still make our sacrifices. We never stopped. We put people to death, but we make an excuse ... they're the bad guys. So Sean doesn't need an excuse to kill; he just does it as an offering to the gods. Maybe ... I could join your church."

She knew she was feeling her way into Sean's brain through Herbert.

"Yeah, I'll tell him. Maybe ..."

"Maybe you won't have to kill me. Is that what you were going to say?"

"But ... oh ... there's the phone. That's him."

He took the phone in the living room where he could keep an eye on her, and still keep the conversation private. She glanced around in search of a weapon.

When he hung up, he had a depressed look in his face.

"He just wanted to check on us. Said they're gettin' ready to go down on the beach. He just parked the pick-up"

"What's the matter?"

"He says you're connin' me. I gotta tie you back up."

"Herbert." She spoke softly, and looked directly into his eyes as if to address something inside of him so tender, it could not be touched, like a fresh wound. When he saw her acceptance and respect, it flowed down into his soul like honey into tea. When it dissolved, his flavor would be changed forever, and she knew it. She was trying to reach him. Of course, she wanted to save her life; but it was not a con ... it was real.

"Whatever you have to do, I understand. I don't want to die ... I won't kid you. I will do whatever I have to do to save my life, even if I have to hurt you."

He broke a dim smile at the thought of this little lady hurting him.

158

"I understand." She said as she walked over to him, and touched his face, the most sensitive part of the man, the part that made people cringe. "I respect your space. You will never see hatred in my eyes, even as you take my life."

His heart sank as if into an abyss, leaving him defenseless. He knew she wanted to convince him to let her go; but what he saw in her face was more than sugar-coated trickery. He had lived on the streets, and knew a con when he saw it; this was no con. She had touched his soul; and, for the first time in his life, he realized he had one.

He had killed before without compunction; yet, he was beginning to wonder about his own intentions. Sexually, he was completely perverted; but the murders ... always with Sean. He didn't want to admit to himself that Sean had used his perverted mind as a tool, had instigated the murders, and exercised complete control over him.

Even as he retied Jenny to the bed, he wondered why. Why was he doing this? Was it really what he wanted?

She was surprised when he tied her wrists loosely. Was he aware of it? He seemed preoccupied, but it could be an invitation. She covered her surprise with a labored expression of nonchalance.

For the first time in his life, he was disgusted with himself. He had caught a glimpse of the real world, where life changed a little at a time, and, one day, you woke up and discovered that it hadn't worked out the way it was supposed to. We think we can impose our scheme of things on nature; in fact, nature toys with us. When we realize this, we have begun to grow up.

Herbert was growing up. Jenny had entered his mind, penetrated his soul, and had given him a new feeling about himself. He walked to the window in the living room, and looked out at the bay below. He could see the south tower of the Golden Gate Bridge.

"He never asked me if I wanted breakfast," Jim said, confused.

"Jim," Jenny whispered as she wiggled her hands, "forget breakfast. I got my hands loose."

"Wow! Do me, quick."

She loosened the ropes, and slithered out of the bed quickly; a snake could not have been more skillful.

"Hurry," Jim whispered. "Get me loose, but, fa' God's sake, don't make any noise. If we blow it, we're screwed."

She whispered as she untied him. "There's a poker near the fireplace. One hit with that, and we're gone."

They kneeled down, and crawled out of the room. From behind a couch, they could see Herbert staring out the window; he seemed to be mesmerized as he watched the weather turn violent.

"There it is," Jenny said as she stared at the poker.

A simple fireplace poker ... the difference between life and death. She became tentative as she thought about Alex. No way could she hit Herbert in the head, she would freeze; but she could hit him in the knees or the shins. As powerful as he was, he could not walk with that kind of hit.

"Let me do it," Jim whispered.

"No. I'm smaller. You might bump things with your square shoulders."

"Are you sure you can do it?"

"Easy. One shot in the shins, and he'll be in so much pain ... cover me. I'll sneak up on his left. In case anything goes wrong, you can distract him from his right."

She crawled so quickly to the fireplace, that she surprised herself. Only problem was, she had to lift the poker out of its holder very quietly. As she did, she heard a very slight tick as the tip touched metal to metal.

Herbert flinched, but did not move; he was twenty feet away. If he had heard it ... she would have to move decisively.

In less than two seconds, she was crouched behind him and to his left. Jim moved in on his right flank as Jenny pulled the poker back from a low stance that any baseball player would be proud of. As she was about to swing, she caught the reflection

160

of Herbert's face in a mirror; he was looking directly into her eyes. She froze ... he froze ... Jim froze. For half a minute, they stood silent and motionless like actors off-stage waiting for their cue.

Finally, Jenny screamed. "Why don't you stop me!" Tears flooded her face.

"You could have killed me."

"You could have stopped me!"

"Why didn't you kill me?"

"Why didn't you stop me? Why!"

Herbert looked at Jim, still frozen in his tracks, eyes wide.

"I'm sorry, Jim." She dropped the poker and her head at the same time. "I couldn't, I just ..."

"It's OK."

"No." Herbert spoke angrily as he turned back to the window. "It's not OK. I'm not OK. I'm ... evil."

Surprised, Jim and Jenny looked at each other with renewed hope.

"No," Jim said timidly, "not if you don't choose to be. It's your choice."

Robert Frauenhofer

Go Daddy

*I*t has been said that Ghandi produced an aura so bright, that it effected everyone in the village, even at a great distance. People felt better, happier, even holier in his presence.

Jenny, always bright, bubbly, wide-eyed, and childlike, effected Herbert, not only sexually, but spiritually, by her very presence.

For Herbert, the world was dark, blacked out by his own form of blindness. When Jenny entered his life, a bright star had turned on, a star like Ghandi himself, and the world was bathed in white light.

In that light, Herbert had made his choice.

A black Mercedes with black interior crossed the bridge from Sausalito carrying an unlikely trio.

"Sean left the keys for me in case I needed it."

"I can see he likes black," Jenny remarked.

"A symbol of evil."

"Why?" Jim tried to understand. "Why would anybody want to stand for evil?"

"I guess ... well, he told me about that once. He said, a tiger eats a gazelle, and ... well, what's good for the tiger is bad for the gazelle."

"I understand," Jenny replied. "But there's more to it than that. Good grows out of evil the way a plant grows into the light. The roots grow in the darkness of ... look!"

"What?"

"Pulling into the toll booth ahead. It's a white '57 ... aghhh! It's mine! That's my car! Follow that Chevy!"

"Wait," Jim cautioned. "Just because it has green plates ..."

"That's my car!"

Herbert followed the car as it turned off the bridge at the first exit. "He's going down the coast."

"No. He's turning. Vista Point."

163

Jenny spoke in disbelief. "With my car. He's playing tourist with my car!"

"Nobody cares anymore," Jim said. "They'll do anything."

The Chevy parked two spaces from the red van, where Don and Candy sat wondering about the experience they'd had. Don questioned his own sanity; but Candy thought about the fun of flying. They watched curiously as a short, porky man got out of the Chevy and walked toward the bridge.

The Mercedes hovered around the parking lot, and stopped next to a tour bus. Jenny revved up with excitement.

"Let me out!"

Jim tried to hold her back. "What are you going to do?"

Herbert held her down as she fought with Jim.

"Let me out!"

"Wait. He might have a gun. At least give him a chance to get out of sight; he's probably making a drug deal out there."

Candy looked over as the trio struggled in the Mercedes.

"Why are they fighting, dad? It's two men against one lady."

"Where?"

"In that black car, over there."

He turned and said, "They're not fighting now; maybe they had an argument." When he turned back, he stared at the Chevy. "That white Chevy looks familiar."

"It was here before. I saw it parked right next to us."

Tourists emerged from the bus and flooded the area. Don wished they would go home and leave the bridge in peace.

"Look, dad!"

Jenny was running through people toward the Chevy with Jim and Herbert in pursuit.

"I've got the key ... my duplicate. Don't stop me!"

She opened the door, and let them in from the driver's side.

"Slide over! Hurry! We're otta here! Yahooo!" She could not hold back her excitement and joy now that she had her car back. As she drove off, she screamed again. "Yahoooo!"

"Dad! Daddy! That's him! That big man! That's the man ..."

"Calm down, Candy. What man. What are you talking about?"

"He was in the truck!"

"What truck?"

"Don't you remember? The truck! I saw Kevin in a truck, and that man was with him. I know it was him, 'cause he's so ugly. Go, daddy ... go!"

Don almost laughed at her words. Go, daddy ... go? She said it again, this time in the strongest duck-quack voice she could muster. "Go, daddy ... go!"

Don started his engine, then hesitated.

"Go, daddy, go!"

He backed out slowly, and looked over at the black Mercedes. Why would they leave the Mercedes, and steal the Chevy? Why did they argue? Why ... oh, hell ... nothing else to do.

"I'm going after that Chevy."

"Yeeaaah! Here we come, Kevin! Go, daddy, goooooooh!"

"OK, settle down. We can't let them know they're being followed."

Tourists scattered as Don drove slowly across the parking lot. He watched the Chevy closely as it moved under the bridge entrance, and headed south.

"They must be going down the coast," Don said calmly, still not convinced that he was doing the right thing.

Herbert thought about the black Mercedes. "Looks like Sean will be getting a parking ticket."

Jim laughed. "Looks like Sean will be getting his car towed."

Jenny smiled. "Looks like you don't care anymore, Herbert."

Jim, sitting in the middle, looked at Jenny, then at Herbert. "Looks like we're a team."

165

"Yeah." Jenny held her right hand out in front of Jim. He grabbed it and held on. Herbert placed his big hand over theirs and said, "A team."

Together they screamed, "Yahoooo!"

"We gotta save that kid." Herbert was anxious to do something good. It would require an inner transformation which few people had ever accomplished. Part of him fought back; another part was afraid as he heard words clearly in his mind, words which recalled a time that felt just like now: 'Throw him in, and walk away. If he learns to swim, he's a survivor. If not, he drowns. Ha, ha, ha.' Two men swung him back and forth as his eyes bulged in fear. 'See ya kid.'

He was plunged into the deep, dark water; but something in him said: I will not die. I will not die! I AM!

Now there was another boy whose life was threatened. Sean had to be stopped, no matter what.

"Do you still have your phone?" Jenny interrupted his thoughts.

"Right here in my pocket. I can talk to Sean anytime."

"This is great. He won't be looking for my '57 Chev."

As she drove slowly down the scenic highway toward Baker Beach, she marveled at the beauty of this place; but Jim and Herbert ignored the scenery as they looked anxiously for the black pick-up.

Gusty winds did not discourage joggers and cyclists from using these beautiful bluffs to express the vitality of life gushing through them. Cypress and Eucalyptus towered above like giant warriors protecting people from the menace of an all consuming ocean. Tourists felt secure under their branches as they gazed down at the water crashing against the rocks.

Herbert sat up, and bumped his head. "There it is! The truck ... in the trees where I figured it would be."

"Go in there." Jim spoke spontaneously without regard for danger.

"But, he ..."

"Don't worry. He won't see us. They must be down below the cliffs."

As she drove off the road, she sneered and said, "I don't know if I like this; you're reading my mind already, and we're not even married."

"Sorry. Park behind ..."

"I know. I will." She drove behind a small building as Herbert looked at them and chuckled. He loved Jenny; but he knew she was in Jim's heart, and he was in hers.

Don watched them park the Chevy and quickly pulled the red van off-road, and parked under a tree. From their slightly higher position, Don and Candy could see the Chevy but not the black pick-up.

"I wonder what they're up to. Why'd they park so close to that building?"

"They're hiding. See? I told you, dad. They're doing something bad."

"They're staring at something ... just the way we're staring at them. I hope they don't see us."

But the trio of potential heroes was intent on watching the pick-up; besides, they had no reason to believe anyone would be following them.

As they sat in waiting, Herbert said, "I'm afraid."

Jim and Jenny looked at him in surprise, but said nothing.

"No, I'm not afraid of what's happening right now; I'm afraid of what's happening right now; I'm afraid of me. I'm ... I'm ..."

"It's OK," Jenny said with great compassion. "You can say it. We're your friends ... we're a team. Whatever you need to say ... say it."

"I'm ... they're right." He swallowed and stared straight ahead. "I'm a ... I'm Herbert the pervert."

Jenny looked past Jim at Herbert's trance-like face. His ugliness seemed to fade as the energy in his eyes sparkled with the beauty of the universe itself.

"Right now, you're a here; you're trying to save a boy's life."

But Herbert knew he was no hero; he knew the awful things that he and Sean had done. It started with the cats ... burn 'em alive. At first, Herbert wanted so bad to save the poor cat as Sean laughed. But, several cats later, Herbert got used to it, and it was easy. Sean deliberately indoctrinated him, and slowly worked up to more heinous crimes. He played to Herbert's perversion, and always reminded him that it was he who had saved him from the streets.

Jim interrupted. "Let me out. I want to go down the trail. Maybe I can see them on the beach below."

"Be careful," Jenny said as Herbert let him out on the passenger side.

Being alone with Jenny instantly sparked Herbert; but he subdued the impulse with a mere glance. She was aware of it, and took his hand. Without looking at her, he said, "I won't let you down."

Jim walked cautiously through the unpaved parking area, and found some trees for cover. He glanced at the pick-up, fifty feet to his left, and continued toward the trail. Gusty winds still punched their way into the bay, but with less power and frequency. He realized that the wind could make it difficult for him to hear someone coming. His neck stretched, as if he had seen something, and he disappeared between shrubs and down the hill toward the beach.

Jenny whispered as if someone could hear. "Careful, Jim."

Don and Candy could not see beyond the parking area where the trail began, and wondered where the young man with the square jaw had gone.

"Maybe this doesn't have anything to do with us."

"Oh, dad. That's the man, and I remember the white car."

"That's just a coincidence." He looked up through the windshield. "I guess this cloud cover is not going to burn off today. Hope it doesn't get foggy."

Suddenly, Jim burst through the shrubs and ran back to the Chevy. Herbert opened the door, and slid to the middle of the seat next to Jenny.

"Here they come! What do we do?"

"He's armed," Herbert said quietly. "Can't take any chances on the boy's life. Sean's crazy. He'll do anything."

Sean held onto Kevin as they emerged from the trail looking tired and angry. He seemed to be scolding Kevin as they hurried back to the truck.

Jenny spoke slowly as she watched. "We'll follow and wait for our chance."

"Yeah," Jim said. "That phone of yours might come in handy. We might be able to figure out a way to distract him at the right time."

Don and Candy watched in confusion, unable to see Sean and Kevin as they returned to the truck. They were like spectators who watched spectators who watched a play.

"I wonder what happened, dad."

"I don't know. He saw something, and ran back to hide in the car."

They wondered no more when the pick-up backed up, churned up rocks and dirt, and sped into the road. Sean turned to the north in the direction of the bridge, unaware of the white Chevy which followed.

As the black pick-up came closer and closer, Don stared at the figure on the passenger side. Suddenly, he felt the hairs stand up on the back of his neck. His eyes opened wider and wider.

"Ohhh ... myyyy ... GOD!"

"Yaaaaaaagghhh!" Candy stood straight up until she jammed her head into the roof. "Kevin! Yaaaaghh!"

Tears gushed from Don's huge eyes, his face crinkled uncontrollably, his body trembled from the top of his head to the soles of his feet.

"My boy. My boy. Oh, Kevin. Oh, Kevin."

"GOOOOOOOOO,   DADDEEEEEEEE, GOOOOOOOOOO!"

He could hardly see through the tears, as he made a U turn into the road without checking the traffic.

Sean had no idea that he was being followed by a white Chevy; nor did Jim, Jenny, or Herbert have a clue that they were being followed by a red van.

Three vehicles, black, white, and red; fitting, symbolic: Evil led the way, good pursued, pain followed.

It was always that way; the Hitlers of the world were our leaders. Why did good always wait for evil to lead the way? Why was it necessary to produce so much pain?

Jim was puzzled. "Where in the hell are they going?"

"Looks like they might end up on Lombard," Herbert said as he crouched down as far as he could. "I better get low just in case."

"I hope you're good in traffic, Jenny."

"I can handle it."

She was exhilarated by the chase. She felt like an actress in one of those movies where the big chase scene always took place on the hills of San Francisco; but, as she drove up Lombard, she realized it couldn't happen here. Traffic was heavy, and she had to work hard to keep up with Sean.

A light turned orange. This was it; if she didn't make it, the pick-up was gone. Anxious cars jammed the intersection ready to pounce when the light changed.

"Punch it!" Jim yelled.

Her heart was pounding in her head as cars pulled into the intersection from right and left. Herbert ducked, horns blasted.

"Oh, shit."

"Damn! I don't believe we made it. You OK?"

"Soon as ..." she swallowed. "Soon as I catch my breath."

"They're heading toward the Marina. Stay with 'im."

Sean drove recklessly, and spoke angrily. "You best not be jackin' me around, kid. I can call Herbie any time, and have your friends snuffed in a heart-beat. I'm beginning to think you have no idea where the money is. That whole trip to the beach was a stall, wasn't it!"

"No. I told you what's happening. I don't understand it, but I see these pictures in my mind. We had to go there first, before we could go to the next place. It's like ... like a movie. We have to go through all the scenes before we ..."

"You better be right."

Things were beginning to come together in Sean's mind. The boy's memory might be coming back to him as he goes from place to place, like going back to a trail where you walked years ago. Each scene refreshes your memory of what you had seen before. It was fate. Yes! Nothing could stop him if the forces of evil worked on his behalf. The boy would lead him to the money so he could fulfill his destiny. Now he could obey his mother's command to be great, to change the world.

It was all so obvious now. His fate was being served by a boy who had a million to one chance to survive a fall like that. It had to be more than coincidence; it was the synchronicity postulated by Jung: all things in the universe work together.

Sean was thrilled. The money would be his.

"Yes," he said with a gleam in his eyes. "Take your time. What do you see now?"

"The grassy ... that way. Go back toward the bridge ... along the water."

Kevin glanced at the kites in the air, but kept his attention riveted to his plan to run into a crowd, and get help as soon as he saw an opportunity. He could have Sean arrested as a kidnapper, and the hostages would have to be released. But, the kites. He frowned and looked back at the sky. "What? That's my ..."

"What? What is it?"

"That's my kite. That's my kite in the air!"

"What the hell are you talking about?"

"That's my ... I built it. I ..." He stopped himself as he was about to say that he remembered everything.

171

Like a transmission that was slipping, and finally grabbed with a clank, his memory suddenly kicked in, and filled his mind with scenes from the bridge.

"What's wrong with you, kid? What do you see?"

He saw himself falling from the bridge in slow motion, the surface of the water coming toward him, and yet ... no fear.

Energy had surrounded the bridge like a bubble; and he had felt like a particle suspended on its surface. It was as if the bubble had popped as he slipped into the water feet first.

Sean was excited as he watched Kevin's trance-like face. "Is it the money? The money? The money!"

"The ... the bridge."

"We're on our way," Sean said eagerly.

Kevin was so astonished by what he remembered, that he did not think to observe who was flying his kite.

Chills pierced Sarah's spine as she suddenly felt the presence of her son. She looked up at the kite and knew that he was looking at it at this very moment. She looked around in desperation; but saw only the blur of heavy traffic in the street. Her heart beat faster as she looked back up to the kite with tears in her eyes and said, "Oh, my God, Kevin. I know you're here. Why don't you come to me? I know you see your kite."

Don had lost sight of the black pick-up; but he managed to keep pace with the white Chevy. He had often said that he could tolerate the traffic in San Francisco, because it was such a great city. Not this time. He was so anxious to get to Kevin, that he did everything in his power to stay with the Chevy, even if he had to ding a few cars to get through.

"Watch out, dad! You just cut that guy right off the road!"

"Sorry, pal, but I can't figure out what's going on here, and nobody stops me until I find out."

He thought about the possibility that Kevin had seen the kite, and was directing the driver of the truck to his mother; but it didn't fit into the puzzle with the Chevy, and the big, ugly guy.

"Wait a minute," he said, confused. "Candy. Didn't you say you saw that big guy in the pick-up?"

"I told you that. He was in the black truck. I know he was."

"And now he's in the white car with somebody else, and they're following the truck ... and they're all heading for the kite. If they keep going ... they did. They drove right by."

"The kite! I see the kite, dad! There she is. There's mom!"

Don sped into the parking lot toward Sarah, and leaned on the horn as Candy waved from the window.

"Mom! Mom!"

Don waved and screamed without letting off the horn. "Yagghhh!"

People were startled, and reacted defensively, but settled back to their fun as Sarah let go of the kite, and ran toward the van.

"Kevin!" She screamed, expecting to see him.

Don jumped out as she sprinted across the field. He held his arms outstretched, and shouted joyfully.

"Kevin is ALIVE!"

She was out of breath as she ran into his arms and squeezed; but he pushed her into the van clumsily.

"Get in, quick. He's in a black truck up ahead. Hurry!"

Tears gushed from her face as he practically threw her in over the driver's seat.

Candy screamed, "Mom! We saw him! He passed right by us. We saw him, mom."

"What?" She wiped her face. "I ... catch my ... breath ... where?"

"It's true. Hang on. I'll explain. What the ..."

"That's them!" A man said as he ran in front of the van. "Stop! You bastards!"

"Get out of my way! I'm warnin' you, I'll run you down!"

"The cops are looking for you!"

When Don saw others coming over to help, he revved the engine, and drove at the man until he forced him to jump out of the way. As they drove into the street, rocks bounced off of the back window.

"Good daddy," Candy quacked.

173

"They're not stopping me from my son ... nothing ..."

"I knew he was alive," Sarah said through tears. "It's just a matter of time now."

"Yeah, if we don't have any more run-ins with those idiots."

He explained about Kevin, while Sarah looked at the sky where the kite, truly a work of art, floated over the bay toward the bridge. The hook seemed to have a mission as it dangled from the end of the string; but it became smaller and smaller, and drifted into the gray sky as if into nothing. It was then that she understood about light: It does not travel through space, it creates space, and, therefore, time. Space and time are non-existent until light expands itself. She wondered why these thoughts entered her mind at a time like this. It was as if the experience of feeling Kevin's presence had opened a door to the unknown. 'And if space does not exist where light has not been, could we not travel from one side of the universe to the other in zero time if we reached out beyond light where time and space do not exist?'

For an instant, she knew the answer; and it was so simple, she was amazed.

Her mind snapped back to the chase.

"We have to be cautious. That man could be trying to help him, or he could be ..."

"I know," Don replied. "And I don't know how those people in the white car are involved; but, no matter what it takes, Kevin ..."

"I know, Don." She put her arm around Candy. "But be careful."

"Look, mom. The kite. It's going toward the bridge."

It was a strange scene. The kite, with a three inch hook attached to the end of the string, looked as if it could latch onto the bridge, and carry it away.

Sarah thought she would never see it again; but, like Angie Skipper's ghost, it would come back to haunt her.

Blood Lust

.

*T*he smell of rubber and exhaust from cars speeding over the bridge was erased by clean ocean winds on their way into the bay.

Tourists didn't like wind, but they were charged by it ... animated. When winds were strong enough, they didn't hear any other sounds, just wind in their ear ... howling ... whistling ... speaking. It was almost like stepping into another dimension, where human voices could not be heard from a world walled off by the wind.

What happened next could have been from a twilight zone 'out there' as people discovered the world of possibility, a world which came from 'in here'.

"Jump! Jump a little!"

"I can't do it."

"Try another spot. That's it. Now jump up. There ya' go! Hold on!"

"Wow! It's like walking on the moon!"

"Are you people crazy? You'll go over the side!"

TV cameras recorded the strangest scenes ever witnessed by the human race: tourists had discovered floating.

Mac Rogers was there to report the incident to his radio listeners "These motorists are not supposed to be stopping like this," he shouted into the microphone, unable to contain his excitement. "If you're listening to me now, and you're on the bridge, please continue. Do not stop."

His plea only made people more curious. Brakes screeched on the bridge as people got out of their cars to watch what they knew could not be happening. Even as thirty people floated up and down, onlookers insisted it was a hoax; but Don and Candy would not doubt the reality of this phenomenon.

Candy couldn't wait to inform her mom of the experience they had had, unaware of the fact that the same thing was happening to others even as she spoke.

175

"Mom. We floated on the bridge! Me and daddy. We ..."

"What!" Sarah looked at Don questioningly.

"It's true. It really happened." Don was focused on the white Chevy, but he felt the need to tell Sarah everything. "Candy ... tell mom what you felt as you were pulled up into the air."

"I felt ... like a tingle ... all over."

"So did I."

Sarah recalled the articles they had read about floaters. "Then it's really true ... just a natural occurrence of some kind. I didn't believe it."

"Yes. I had goose bumps all over. The earth's electromagnetic field must have shifted as the earth wobbled, just like they said. Could a concentration or ... or ... alignment of magnetic lines somehow ... create anti-gravity?"

Don pulled into the right lane. "They're heading toward the bridge. Watch close. If they get off at Vista Point, we'll have to make that quick right. If we miss it, we're stuck. We'd have to go over the bridge. I can't see the black truck ... too much traffic."

Cars moved slower until they dropped into a stop-and-go mode. Those who listened to Mac Rogers on the radio were anxious to get to the bridge, and tail-gated or switched lanes.

Sarah was worried. She thought about crime and kidnapping; a boy could disappear, and never be found. Cops can't keep up with it anymore; they wouldn't even take it seriously. They wouldn't believe he was still alive after a fall like that. "What's going on? This traffic is getting out of hand. Something must have happened!"

"Click on the radio."

Mac continued to describe the scene to his listeners. "There it is before your very eyes, if you're watching TV, or if you're listening to me on ... look at that. My God! Don't they realize they could go over? Somebody needs to stop this. For those of you listening now, I can tell you, this is not a hoax. These people are like astronauts on the moon, only more so. Just a little jump, and they're off. Gravity has somehow been ... lady! Oh, God. She's coming back down, and her dress is in her face. The guys are really getting a show; but she dare not let go of the cable."

Don and Sarah stared at each other as they listened; the traffic was at a stand-still.

Candy broke in with, "I guess they won't call us liars now, ay, dad?"

He spoke softly, as if in reverence. "That place is packed with energy."

"Energy," Sarah said calmly. "Energy from people."

Don looked at Sarah and spoke submissively as if to apologize for all the teasing about Sarah's secret. "Where two or more are gathered in my name, there am I. You said that."

"Yes." She accepted his apology; she knew he understood now.

"They've stopped it." Mac said, relieved. "They put a stop to it. The cops are moving the traffic again, and they're clearing the bridge of pedestrians. Thank God. I thought for sure I would witness a horrible fall into the bay."

As traffic started moving again, Sarah spoke nervously. "They're getting close, Don. I see the white car. He's slowing down."

"That's it! Vista Point!"

"But the place is packed. Why would they go there?" She was confused. "Don't they realize what's happening?"

"Probably have no idea." Don spoke slowly and thoughtfully. "Must be a reason. I don't know what Kevin is involved in; but I bet it has to do with ... thirteen million dollars."

"Oh, Don. Don't be ridiculous. How much trouble can he get into in one ... yes. You're right. Kevin I'm gonna spank your ..."

"Oh, mom."

"Only Kevin could do this. Who else would ... the kite ... the bridge ... now ... who knows what? I'll kill him. So help me ..."

Don smiled. "The only way you'll kill him is if you squeeze him to death when you hug him."

"Hug-a-bugga. I can't wait. God, don't let anything happen to him. Please, God, let us get him back safely."

Don joked through his nervousness. "Why? So you can kill him?" He bumped the curb as he turned off the highway, and caught a glimpse of the truck just as it turned toward Vista Point; the white Chevy was only two car-lengths behind.

Traffic was heavy, but most cars were leaving as police directed cars away from the parking lot. A policeman stopped the red van.

"Hold it, Sir. Can't go in."

Don lost it. "What! But those cars got in just ahead of me."

"No more. You'll have to go straight." He pointed down the road which led back to Fort Point under the bridge. "That way, sir."

"But you don't understand! My son is in that pick-up going in there!"

"You'll have to park down the street, sir."

"But this is a matter of ..."

The cop walked away, and stopped another car.

"Just go, Don! Do what he said; but as soon as we're out of sight, park anywhere. Let 'em give us a ticket. We'll double park if we have to!"

All three heads looked back toward the bridge as Don drove in a panic. He was getting too far away from his son.

As the rear-view mirror filled with cars, he yelled, "I can't stop! There's too many cars behind me!"

"We're too far away. My Kevin. Stop! Let me out!" Sarah opened the door before he could stop. She jumped out and held onto the open door with her feet off the ground as the van screeched to a halt. "I'll see you up there!"

"Mom!"

"Stay there!" she ordered.

She disappeared up the hill between cars. People looked at her in disbelief. Her speed could only be possible for one whose adrenaline was pumping full blast.

"It's OK, Candy," Don said, breathing heavily. "We'll go down to the fort, and we'll walk up the hill to the bridge. We'll go up the path. It takes us right there ... to Vista Point. We'll meet mom there."

"And Kevin."

"And those guys ... and the ... big ugly guy." The more Don thought about it, the more he realized how dangerous it could be.

"What are we gonna do, dad?"

"We'll think of something."

As they approached the old fort, his memory suddenly exploded with a scene so clear, he could almost see it projected on the building in front of him.

"That big guy ... he's the one who ... he stopped me when I tried to go after Kevin in the water ... near the fort. Why didn't I realize that?"

"You were upset, dad."

"Yes. And coming back here made me remember."

"Dad ... who's ... the good guys? Dad?"

Don did not answer.

"Is that big ugly guy the bad guy? Dad, what's mom gonna do? I'm scared."

"Don't worry, she can take care of herself."

This was her place, her bridge, and it beckoned to her as the late afternoon sun beamed across the water under the canopy of clouds that covered the bay. The San Francisco skyline appeared remote under the gray sky, while the bridge alone flashed and gleamed from the light of the sun.

Newcomers sometimes remarked that the bridge was not gold, it was orange. At this moment, it was gold. It didn't just shine; it lit up like a light bulb, turned on by the energy which had been deposited there by the millions of people who had admired this accomplishment, this vital force which lived in the hearts of men, this entity which breathed with the spirit of those who had turned a dream into reality.

Candy looked up at the bridge over the fort. "Look, dad!"

"Wow!" Don stared at the awesome spectacle. "I've never seen it light up like that. My God ... it's ... lit up. Almost like it's ... fluorescent."

As he parked the van, he almost forgot about his reason for being there. "You can almost hear it."

Candy opened the door to get out. "Listen." She froze. "It's ... humming."

Don got out of the van, and stood in reverence. "It's speaking ... like it's the vocal chords of the earth saying ... I am."

At that moment, Jenny stared at the bridge from the Chevy and said, "It's gold ... it's really gold."

"Yes," Herbert said, spellbound.

Jim agreed. "Something strange is happening here."

Light reflecting from the bridge beamed across the gray sky with the magic of a full moon on a dark night. As the sky darkened further, the beams of light became sharply defined. Alcatraz Island stood directly in the path of a "moonbeam" from the bridge, and appeared to be sliced in half, one side in the light, the other side so dark it seemed to be gone.

It was a sight which made every tourist gaze in awe. They stood in silence, mesmerized, as they focused on the bridge.

But Sean felt nothing as he grabbed Kevin by the hand with an iron grip, and pulled him from the pick-up. He would not let go of his fate, no matter what; he pulled Kevin toward the bridge in anticipation.

"The money's here! Am I right, kid?" His voice, usually, soft, measured and controlled, became loud and wild, as if another spoke through him. "Am I right, kid? Ah, ha, ha, ha! It's here, kid, it's here. I can tell by the look on your face. You know it!"

He leaned over in front of Kevin, looked directly into his eyes, and danced happily. It's here, kid, it's here. Sere kid, tsere! Sere kid, tsere. Ha, ha, ha, ha."

The trio watched from the Chevy only fifty feet away, not concerned that they might be seen; it was obvious that Sean was in a state of agitation which occupied all of his attention.

"Lead on, kid. Lead me to it or I'll blow your brains out right here and now, so help me."

Kevin wondered why he had suddenly become so desperate; was he crazy enough to do it with all these people around? What Kevin didn't know was that Sean had spotted the big man in the white Chevy, and knew immediately that he had been betrayed.

BETRAYAL

DISOBEDIENCE

Words which pushed buttons in Sean's mind, and turned him into a mad-man. He didn't care about the risk now; he only knew, if the money was here, he would not leave without it.

"You won't survive another fall, kid. I'll throw you over myself if I don't get the money. Move!"

Kevin looked up at the south tower.

"What are you looking at?"

As he turned to look, Sean became aware of the strange behavior of the crowd. "What the hell's going on in this place? What are they looking at?"

"The ... the bridge."

"No. Even tourists don't look at a bridge like that. Something must have happened."

Clouds moved over the sun, and the bridge returned to it's normal, everyday glory. Like a chameleon hiding from its prey, it seemed to change colors as soon as Sean looked at it.

Tourists stood around and talked about the amazing things that had happened before their very eyes, as if it were all part of a spectacular show that had made their day. They could go back home and tell friends that they had seen the real Golden Gate Bridge, not just the illusion others had seen. But who would understand?

As police investigated the area where floaters had sailed, cars were allowed to cross as usual; but several cops stood in the middle of the road to make sure that traffic flowed smoothly. When rubber-neckers slowed down, they waved them on and yelled, "Move it! Move it!"

Mac Rogers was allowed to report from the gift shop where he had a view of tourists in the parking area, and the police on the bridge. He spoke with intensity, anxious to understand the strange events which had occurred.

"A scientist has arrived on the scene to check the area; but, from here, it looks like he has not been successful in his attempts to float. He has tried to jump from every position he could on the bridge, and nothing happens. It seems to be back to normal. In fact, it looks like ... yes, they're letting the tourists back on the bridge. That's a surprise. But the cops are staying. They'll not let it happen again. Sir! Officer! Stand by folks. Officer! Can I have a minute? Can you tell us what's happening?"

"Mac? You must be big Mac. Mac Rogers?"

"I confess."

"I listen to you all the time. Didn't know what you looked like."

"Thank you. I'm always pleased to meet a distinguished member of the law."

"Well, I don't know about that distinguished part. I'm just a cop."

"No, not *just* a cop. Besides, if you listen to me all the time, you must be distinguished. But, can you tell us why they ..."

"Ya know somethin' ... you're right. People who listen to you really are distinguished. I think you're right on target. As a cop who sees ... everything, I can tell you, if we don't rebuild the cities ... I mean, really rebuild ... not just beautify ... this country is in the toilet. I support your pyramids."

"Well, I thank you for that. Can you tell us why they decided to let the people back on the bridge?"

"I guess they've decided there is no danger. But we have orders to guard the bridge, especially ... the hot spot ... twenty-four hours a day."

"What about the tourists?"

"They're welcome. The mayor had decided not to deprive tourists, while the scientists figure it out."

"Thank you, sir, for your time, and your words of encouragement. It means a great deal to me. There you have it, folks. You're welcome on the bridge; but please don't ... mess around. And if you drive across, move quickly. There's nothing to see."

Nothing to see ... just the bridge, and happy tourists. The real Golden Gate Bridge was no longer visible; but Sean could not have seen it even if it were.

As they walked on the bridge, now heavily crowded, Sean warned, "Look, kid, if you and your friends want out of this alive, it's real simple. When I know where it's at, you're free; warn the cops, and you leave me no choice. Make it easy for everybody."

As they disappeared into the crowd, the trio emerged from the Chevy and followed cautiously: Jenny, in the middle, held hands with both Jim and Herbert. It was typical Jenny; she turned isolation and animosity into intimacy and acceptance through a simple, innocent act like holding hands.

People did a double-take as they walked by ... a pretty young lady holding hands with a square-faced young man, and a very large, very ugly goon. Some wondered what kind of relationship they must have been into.

Jenny looked to Herbert for assurance. "Can you see them? What can we do in this crowd? We can hardly get through. Maybe we should just tell the cops."

"Can't risk it. Cops might spook him. Sean's psycho. He might do ... anything. Just let me get my hands on him."

"What about us?" Jim asked. "What will you tell him?"

"Uh ... I ..."

"We'll stay back," Jenny volunteered. "Tell him we got away."

Jim didn't like it. "He won't buy it. He know Herbert could have called him. And how would he have known Sean was here on the bridge?"

Jenny thought out loud. "By the time he figures it out, Herbert could have him by the neck."

"But the cops," Jim said as he stopped behind a group of tourists. "They could handle it."

"Not in this crowd. He's too dangerous."

Herbert agreed. "Sean. You don't know him. He would kill the boy, and who knows how many people. You know how many rounds he could get off in a few seconds with that ..."

"Yeah," Jenny said as she peeked through heads in the crowd. "He could cause a panic. Dead cops and a few shots would turn this place into a stampede."

"Not only that," Herbert confessed reluctantly, "there's something else ... worse."

"Worse?"

He whispered. "The bomb."

"Bo-umph." Herbert muzzled her with a big hand.

"Don't say it out loud." He removed his hand as tourists looked on curiously. "One of Sean's sparks climbed down under the bridge and planted it before he jumped. Everybody thought it was just an innocent suicide ... didn't know he planted a ..."

"Innocent suicide?"

"Well ... you know what I mean."

"We have to do something," Jim said as Jenny saw the warrior in him coming out. "We can't tell anybody about the ... panic button ... got to do it ourselves."

Jenny weighed the circumstances quickly in her mind. "With Herbert's strength ... let him take him. We can stay behind people ... get as close as we can, and pull the boy away at the last ..."

"Jenny, no. I'll go."

"I can ..."

"No!" Jim interrupted angrily.

"It's a free country."

"No! Period!"

"Jim, we're not married yet."

"No!" He stared into her eyes, and she knew, once and for all, no meant no.

"Are you two done fightin'?"

"Yes!" Jim said, still staring at Jenny.

She acquiesced as Jim and Herbert worked their way into the crowd; but as they disappeared into people, she felt an urge to follow. She would not miss the action regardless of the risk, a risk much greater than she could imagine.

Mac Rogers had walked back to the bridge, still in contact with the station.

"The people are calm and orderly now; but the crowd has grown enormously. They're curious ... uh ... little bump and shove there ... but the cops have it under control. Oh."

"What is it, Mac? What's happening?"

"That's her ... the lady who lost her boy. She's coming toward us. What's she doing here again?"

As Sarah approached, a man yelled, "That's her! She's back! My God, lady. How can you have the nerve to come back here looking for the money after what happened. Stop her! She's a murderer!"

"Wait!" Mac stepped in front of Sarah to defend her.

"You're that whacko pyramid guy!" a lady shouted.

"He's in it with her. Why else did they meet here like this?"

"Get her!"

"No!" Sarah screamed. "He's alive! My son is alive! He's here!"

An angry-faced man rushed Mac and pushed, head first like a bull, knocking him to the ground.

What Sarah lacked in strength, she made up for with courage. She fought fiercely as Mac jumped to his feet, and fought people back.

"Murderer! Help! Murderer!"

"Please! My boy! Kevinnn! Ugh."

Blood gushed forth, the crowd stopped, a knife hit the ground with a clank.

Sarah looked down at the puddle of blood ... it was hers. She fell as somebody ran off, unseen by the crowd who stared in horror.

"Stop the bleeding!"

A young woman emerged from the crowd, topless, carrying her blouse. "Here, take this."

Mac knelt down next to Sarah supporting himself with one hand covered with blood as the young woman wrapped her thigh with the blouse. In the scuffle, the attacker had missed his mark and tore the flesh above her right leg.

"I'm fine. Let me up."

"You need a doctor."

"No." She pulled herself up on one leg.

"Sarah!" Don pushed his way through the crowd. "Oh my God. What happened?"

"I'm OK. Just go! This crowd is crazy ... it's a lynch mob. They called me a murderer. Where's Candy?"

"I had to leave her in the van."

"Oh, Don."

"I had no choice. She'll be OK."

"Hurry."

"But your leg."

"Just go."

They moved quickly as the crowd stood, sobered by the blood of an innocent woman.

The topless woman watched with amazement as Sarah limped off with the bloody blouse around her leg.

"Don't you wear a bra, lady?"

"Yeah, don't just stand there, indecent."

Mac stood up and addressed the crowd. "Is that all you can think of? It's just sex and blood, ain't it?" He spoke as if to himself. "Blood lust, that's what it is." He raised his bloody hands and said, "Here ... lick it. Isn't that what you want?"

They stared in silence as cops arrived on the scene.

Mac reported the incident to the station, but his heart was not in it. Sadness dripped from his voice as he said, "Ladies and gentlemen ... more madness ... here on the bridge. People become mobs at the drop of a hat. I feel like ... this is not the world I grew up in. But I still support the concept of the pyramid city. I still believe we can figure out a way to live in peace. Mankind ... the most ... supposedly the most intelligent species ... we can do it."

But he wondered if he was just naive as Daryl had said. Was the human race beyond all hope?

He would soon know.

"Your leg." Don said as he held on to her. "Are you sure you can make it?"

"It's fine. Just ... tore it up ... bloody, but not ... he's here!" she said through tears.

"Sarah, no. Let me find him. You go back."

"No. A mother ... when she's this close to her son ..."

Don scolded jokingly. "Now you cry ... now that you know he's alive."

"I knew it all along, but now we're getting close. I ... can't help it."

He comforted her and helped as she limped along, but did nothing further to discourage her. "These people ... where did they all come from? Stay behind me! I'll push our way through!"

Sarah saw an opening. "Follow that big guy. They're getting through."

"That's ... that's him ... the big ugly guy. He's after Kevin!"

"Don prepared himself; he would fight to the death if need be. Nothing would keep him from his son.

"Kevinnnnnn!"

Robert Frauenhofer

Falling Bridges

Sean did not know how close Herbert and Jim were. His high-pitched voice betrayed a feeling of desperation. If Herbert had turned on him, he could lose everything ... his organization, his destiny.

"Well, kid, it's your choice, live or die. You know where it's at."

"Yes ... I do."

"Where!"

"Up there." Kevin looked up.

"What? How could it be up there?"

"It's there."

Sean stared up at the bridge ... of course ... the riddle ... the top shelf. He thought about the workmen who walked the great cables; only a handful of men were allowed up there through an elevator inside the tower. Somehow, Zack Pinches must have gained access to the elevator. If it was there, Sean would never get to it. No wonder treasure hunters could not find it. As he turned back toward Kevin, he saw Herbert's ugly head bobbing above the dense crowd.

A fat belly bumped into kevin, and he realized immediately that his opportunity had arrived. He dived head first between the belly and a large set of floppy boobs, and snaked his way into the crowd; he was free! But a hand reached through bodies, and grabbed him by the arm. He turned and tried to pull himself loose.

"Don't worry. Just keep moving." It was Jenny.

Sean glanced at a cop in the road, and back to the ugly head coming closer; he knew it was over. He struggled to the rail and climbed on it as Herbert pushed his way toward him.

Herbert bellowed, "I'll tear your arms off!"

As he grabbed at his heels, Sean climbed a vertical cable. Herbert started to climb after him, but Jim screamed, "No! You'll be killed! Noo! The boy! Get the boy!"

"Nothing's gonna stop me!" Sean screamed as he looked down at Herbert. He pulled a small transmitter from his jacket. "Remember this?"

"Oh, my God."

"What is it?" Jim looked at the horror in Herbert's face.

"The bomb. He's gonna blow the bridge. The ... the center span."

"Bomb!" A woman screamed. "Bomb! Bomb!"

Jenny pushed Kevin away as sheturned back to find Jim. "Go ahead! Find your mom!"

A wave of people gushed toward Don and Sarah who held onto the rail. Kevin seemed to ride the wave, his feet lifting off the ground, carried by push and shove.

"Mom!"

"Kevin!" This was the first she had seen of him since the fall; she couldn't hold back the tears.

Don reached for him, but he surfed past them on heads and shoulders.

Cops stopped all traffic as people ran into the road to get away. When motorists saw the stampede, and heard the word, bomb, they tried to back up or make a U turn. When they failed, they abandoned their cars, and ran from the bridge.

Only Jim and Herbert stayed and watched as Sean climbed. When he reached the great round suspension cable, he pulled himself over the top where non-skid paint provided perfect traction. With a small cable on each side to hang on to, he discovered that it was easier to walk the cable than he had thought; but the gusty winds could throw him over in a second.

Mac Rogers climbed to the roof of the gift shop and used binoculars.

"Yes, John, I'm still here. Ladies and gentlemen, this is ... it's madness. I'm sorry ... I'm out of breath. This place is like a focal point. First, floaters, then a young woman ... stabbed ... now ... a stampede ... of people. People being crushed ... a bomb, they say. A man ... wait ... he's on the bridge. I can see him through my binoculars. He ran up the cable ... he's on top

190

of the south tower. Oh ... a kite is floating right near him. It seems to be hooked onto something."

At that moment, Sean bent down and reached between two steel plates where he had seen a black object. He pulled a suitcase, then another.

He had found it ... his destiny!

His mind drifted in and out of the reality he could not bear to see; he was home again, speaking softly, trying not to giggle. "I did it, mom. I did it."

Suddenly, like a cat's claws, the hook on the kite caught his shirt. As he turned in surprise, a powerful gust of wind swept him off his feet.

Police, in a helicopter assigned to investigate, took pictures as they approached. It was a bizarre scene which would later be seen by viewers all over the world.

Sean, in his frenzy, would not let go of the suitcases, one in each hand. As he fell from the tower, he held his arms out as if he were trying to fly. The kite remained hooked to his shirt, and provided a tail. But the suitcases bumped the bridge, and popped open leaving a trail of bundled hundred dollar bills behind him.

Herbert watched as Sean fell into the bay still holding onto the handles. He had caught a glimpse of his glaring face as he fell directly in front of him.

For a moment, Mac was unable to speak as he watched.

Then a voice screamed, "Money! It's the money!"

"They tricked us! It wasn't a bomb; it was the money!"

Don and Sarah were still struggling on the bridge when Kevin worked loose from the crowd and rushed toward them. The crowd seemed to follow as they ran back for the money.

Mac shouted. "It's pandemonium out there! The crowd has reversed direction. Cops or no cops, there's money everywhere, and they want it! This is crazy. They can't keep it. But ... then again, they out number the cops.

"Oh ... fights! Fights have broken out! Oh, my God. He punched ... a guy punched a lady right in the face. A man ... oh ... ladies and gentlemen ... I've never seen anything like this. It makes you lose all faith in the human race. A man fell into the bay before our very eyes, and we fight ... over money. Nobody cares. Cops are trying to stop it, but ... oh, shit."

There was a long silence as Mac stared in disbelief.

"They've turned into animals. A group has jumped on top of a policeman. They got his stick. They're ... they're beating him. They're beating the snot out of him."

For the first time since its birth, people were oblivious to the beauty and grandeur of the bridge. It might have been described as a war zone; but it was a war between individuals ... every man for himself.

Kevin ran into the arms of Don and Sarah. They squeezed each other so hard that Don could hardly speak.

"Now I get my ... hugga-bugga."

"Oh, mom, you're bleeding. Oh, mom ..."

"It's nothing ... just ... just my heart. Ha, ha, ha, ha." Tears covered her face as blood oozed through the blouse and ran down her leg.

The war around them could have been a play where, as theater-goers, they ignored the romping and madness on stage.

But Jim was intensely involved as he climbed onto the rail where a Channel Seven news helicopter hovered just fifty feet away, cameras trained close-up on the action. He grabbed onto a cable, and looked over the crowd for Jenny. Like a sea gull on it's perch, he had a clear view of the entire bridge.

He saw a woman holding a fist full of money as a man ran up behind her.

"Watch out!"

The man leaped in the air, feet first, and kicked her in the back. She hit the pavement with a crash, unconscious, as blood splashed from her face.

In his concern for Jenny, Jim passed over the incident; it made him feel callous. He saw Kevin reunited with his parents, expecting her to be nearby, but she was nowhere in sight. Why did he leave her alone? Stupid. Stupid.

"Where are you?"

He jumped from the rail and stepped on money as he rushed from the bridge.

"No you don't, buddy. That's mine."

Jim punched the man in the face to get through.

"Not bad," he thought. Jenny would be proud. But, as he started to run, a cop pushed him against the rail. "Hey! Not me. I didn't do anything."

Jim kicked him in the balls before he could swing his stick; he fell to his knees and grabbed Jim's ankle. Jim pulled his other foot back, ready to kick, but hesitated. Kicking cops went against his nature; but he could not break the iron grip.

"Jenny! I gotta find her!"

Suddenly, like an automatic reaction from a tap to the 'funny bone', his leg bounced up and pushed his foot into the cop's face.

When he heard the crack of teeth and bone, Jim froze; he wanted to stay and help.

"What have I done? I didn't mean it." He pushed through the crowd as blood gushed from the broken nose and teeth.

"Jenny!" He ran into the road between parked cars, their doors still open, and climbed onto the roof of a white limo. "Jenny! You gotta see me up here."

He had an awful feeling in his stomach, but he didn't want to listen to it.

"The Chevy. She's in the Chevy waiting for me."

He jumped off the roof and ran toward the parking lot, uninterrupted by anyone; only parked cars blocked his run. The crowd was near the center of the bridge fighting for money, except for Don, Sarah, and Kevin who still hugged near the rail above Fort Point.

Kevin looked out between his parents arms and saw his kite rising up from the bay. He jerked loose from their embrace.

"My kite!"

He dodged right and left to get through people running from the bridge with their take.

"No! Kevin! Don, stop him."

"Kevin!" Don yelled, running after him. "If you live through this, I'll kill you."

He reached over the rail and grabbed the string before Don could stop him. Sarah felt her heart pounding, and almost fainted as Don pulled him off the rail.

"I got it! I got it, dad!"

Don was about to chew him out when he was stunned by a strange scene. Sean was floating just beyond the bridge. He seemed to slip around as if he were on top of a huge bubble. Herbert was shocked and angry that Sean was still alive. He ran to Kevin's side, prepared to protect him.

Sean held the transmitter in his hand with a finger over the button.

"No!" Herbert jumped onto the rail, and held onto a cable as he reached out. "Give me your hand! I'll pull you back in!"

"Trust you? Ha, ha, ha, ha."

"It won't last!" Don shouted. "The bubble. It won't hold. You'll fall!"

"And you're going with me. Ahhhh, ha, ha, ha!"

He pushed the button just as the bubble of energy burst, plunging him into the bay.

The blast shot straight up through the center of the bridge throwing bodies in every direction; cars and people dropped into the treacherous waters below.

When the dust settled, cameras showed a thirty foot hole ringed by twisted metal and chunks of concrete. From a distance, the hanging metal and rebar looked almost like the net of a basketball hoop.

A young woman hung on to the net, screaming for help, as others ran from the bridge still holding money in their hands.

Don held onto Kevin who held onto his kite as a wave of people ran by. When he heard the woman screaming, Don ran out toward the hole.

"Dad, no!"

"Gotta see what I can do. Stay there!"

Sarah ran up to Kevin, and held him down to make sure he stayed.

Don walked cautiously toward the edge of the hole, as the bridge moaned and swayed with the pain of a great wound. He knew the wind could blow him over, so he laid down, and crawled to the edge where he looked down at the woman hanging on for her life. He reached down as far as he could, but to no avail.

Jim ran to the scene in a panic.

"No, Jenny ... please ... don't be down there." He slid to the edge almost going too far into the gaping hole. "Jenny!"

Without thinking, he slammed his body over the edge as an extension for Don.

"Hold my feet! Hang on, Jenny! Just a little longer!"

But her eyes told him she could not. As she lost her grip, the terror in her face was more than he could bear. Better to die than to live with that. He lunged down in desperation and grabbed her hand hoping for a miracle. Don grabbed his ankles just in time as Sarah and Kevin ran to his aid. They had formed a human chain, but the links were slipping over the edge one by one.

Herbert suddenly dived into the pavement and grabbed Kevin's ankles. He pulled until his great strength was stretched to the max. Now the chain moved back onto the bridge, link by link.

Jenny's face lit up with a child-like smile as they pulled her up.

"Let's get out of here before this whole section goes!"

Don, Sarah and Kevin hurried down the hill to the van where Candy greeted them excitedly.

Jim and Jenny left arm in arm as rescue crews arrived by land, air and sea.

Herbert was on his own now, alone once again. He watched the happy couple, and waved.

Jenny stopped and looked at Jim. He thought for a moment, then said, "I got lotsa' room in Bolinas."

"Yesss!" She beckoned to Herbert; but he hesitated until Jim waved him on.

"Come on. Come on!"

Like a rejected child who had just been invited to play with the neighborhood kids, Herbert's eyes lit up, and he ran to their embrace.

Mac Rogers spoke with great sadness.

"Many of you have come to join me in our crusade to build a city within a city ... the only sane thing to do. Too ambitious? Not enough leadership to do it? Maybe. But one question I cannot answer: ... am I naive to suggest we can do it? Do people really want to live in harmony ... or do they want ... blood?

"For those of you who are ready to join the cause, I cannot ask you to risk everything to build a great future when your fellow ... beings ... are bent on destruction and murder.

"Maybe ... maybe the answer is nature's way ... Armageddon ... then, start all over again.

"If there is a great leader out there to show the way, I wish he ... or she ... would emerge soon ... before it's too late."

The Pooch

"*T*ell it, dad. Come on."

"Well, we have enough time, that's for sure. By the time we get home ... over the San Rafael and back down ..."

"Candy will be asleep by the time you finish."

"No I won't, mom."

"Are you sure about your leg?"

"Yes. The first aid kit worked perfect, antiseptic and all."

"Come on, dad."

"Well, the only problem is, it's not really the secret of life. I know better now. But I'll tell it anyway. Let's see if I remember. It's about a young man who wanted to continue his education to become a doctor; but he was very adventurous, and wanted to see the world.

He went out to Bodega Bay, and sat down on a cliff overlooking the ocean to ponder his dilemma. If he stayed in school, who knows when he would get a chance to roam. He might die in an accident, and never realize his dream.

"Just then, a golden retriever walked up beside him, and sat down with his back up against his side.

'Well, you sure are a friendly pooch. Where did you come from?'

Don spoke in a deep voice: "'The dog answered, I've been here all along.'

"The young man was amazed. 'Oh, my God. You talked.'"

The dog said, 'Right on both counts. I talked, and I'm God.'

'I must be going crazy,' the young man said.

'And I can help you with your problem. You must stay in school.'

The young man was amazed. 'You really are God,' he said. 'You read my mind. But, Lord ... I want to see the world. What if I die before I ever get a chance?'

197

"And the pooch said, 'I guarantee you will live to be one hundred years old, and still have youth, vitality, strength and energy.'

'Oh, God, thank you. Now I can go back to school. This is great!'

'But there is one catch. You must find the secret of life.' And the pooch disappeared.

"Well, the young man went to school, and became a doctor, hung a shingle ..."

"Hang a shingle?" Candy smiled.

"He opened up his own office. Then he made lots of money, and finally traveled all over the world. In his travels, he searched everywhere for the secret, but couldn't find it.

"Finally, when he was one hundred years old ... and didn't look a day over thirty ... he went back to Bodega Bay and sat down on the cliff. When the pooch appeared, he said, 'I'm sorry, God. I could not find the secret.'

'In that case,' the pooch said in a deep voice, 'I will give you another two hundred years to find it.'

"And he disappeared. Well, the young man ... the young-*old* man was all excited. This was fantastic. Two hundred years. He could do anything he wanted.

"He explored the world beyond his wildest dreams ... even lived in different countries, and learned many languages. His adventures included sky diving, mountain climbing, and deep-sea diving. He bought an airplane, and roamed the world, free as a bird.

"Finally, after the two hundred years were up, he went back to Bodega Bay prepared to die. When the pooch sat down and snuggled against him, he put his arms around him and patted him on the head.

"Lord ... I have failed; I have not discovered the secret of life. And he gave the pooch a hug-a-bugga."

"Oh, dad. He did not. That's not part of the story."

"You're right, Candy. Just wanted to see if you were still awake."

"Come on, dad."

"Well ... the pooch put his nose up against the young-old man's nose and said, 'Then I will give you another five hundred years.' And the pooch disappeared.

"So then, the young man ... who wasn't young, but still looked young ... tried harder than ever to find the secret. If he would find it, he must learn as much as possible. He went back to school, and learned everything about everything ... he had plenty of time. He became an astronomer, then a biologist, then covered all the sciences. When that didn't work, he studied all the religions of the world. Somebody, somewhere had to have the answer.

"He became a lawyer, a judge, a senator, a wealthy businessman ... he even became the richest man in the world. Still no secret. Finally, he gave away everything he had, and lived in the streets as a bum. Then he worked as a laborer, a carpenter, a plumber ..."

"Why would he give away all that money?"

"Candy," Sarah scolded, "don't jump up and down."

"So then," Don continued, "he went back to Bodega Bay after five-hundred years, and sat down overlooking the ocean. The pooch sat down next to him, and put his nose against his nose, and said, 'Try again. This time ... one thousand years. See ya' kid.' And he disappeared.

"He couldn't believe it. Another one thousand years to find the secret of life. This time, he started a foundation dedicated to the pursuit of spiritual growth and awareness, and invited all of the great religious leaders of the world. But even their wisdom failed him.

"After hundreds of years, he was bored and depressed. Then he had an idea. He decided to build a laboratory, and hire the best brains in the country to help him develop a pill."

"A pill? Dad. You're silly."

"But this pill would erase all the memory and knowledge stored in his brain; he would start all over again like a child."

"Why would he do that?"

"Because he read that you must become as a child again to enter the gates of heaven. Maybe with a fresh start and an open mind, he would find the secret. Everything else had failed.

"Finally, the pill was ready; tests on animals proved it worked. He took the pill, and remembered nothing. He had to go to school from the first grade."

"A grown-up in first grade?"

"That's right, Candy. He had to learn everything all over again.

"Well, after twenty years, he happened to be driving up the coast when he decided to stop at Bodega Bay. He was worried about something: he wanted to continue his education and become a doctor; but he felt the urge to explore the world first. So he sat down on a cliff overlooking the ocean as he pondered over the dilemma.

"A golden retriever walked up to him and sat down.

'Hi, pooch', he said. 'Where did you come from?"

'I've been waiting for you.'

'Oh, my God! You talked!'

'Of course,' the pooch said. 'Don't you remember?'

'Remember what?'

"The pooch looked at him with a sparkle in his eyes and said, 'Then I will leave you now, for I see that you have found the secret.'

'Secret? What secret? I don't know anything about a secret.'

"And the pooch disappeared."

There was a long silence before Candy said, "Dad, is that it? Is that the end?"

"No, Candy. There is no end."

Kevin tugged at his arm. "But dad ..."

"What Kevin?"

"You said, it's NOT the secret. So what is?"

"The secret? It's Sarah's secret. She knew it all along. 'When you make the inner as the outer, and when you make the above as the below ... then shall you enter the Kingdom of Heaven.'"

"But..."

"Shh. QUIET!" Sarah had just turned on the radio to get the latest about the bridge. What they heard made their hearts pound with fear.

"NO!" Sarah covered her face and wept.

Don pulled off the road and stopped as he whispered, "No, please God. No."

The voice spoke with tremendous grief. "I repeat, for those of you who may think this ... is ... just ... I ... repeat. This is not ... a hoax . Terrorists have succeeded in ... the ... ultimate. A nuclear bomb ... has exploded in the heart of ... Manhattan. I re ... I ... Oh, God."

Robert Frauenhofer

About The Author

Obsessed with the failings of the superstructure, the author has advocated a better way for 30 years. In Zen Ducks, he establishes, in fiction form, his basic philosophy for a **new way of thinking**.

A long time Zen enthusiast, his favorite writers are **Allen Watts** and **Herman Hesse**. After 2 years at Ohlone College, he left with the impression that he had to make a contribution. But the message of Zen Ducks is so profound, it borders on the mystical. Thus, he has been a reluctant author until now.